ISBN-13: 978-0-578-19152-2
ISBN-10: 0-578-19152-0

Dedicated to my mother.

Other Books and Short Stories

By

Vivienne Diane Neal

Making Dollar$ And Cent$ Out Of Online Dating

Shades of Deception

Malicious Acts

Wicked Intent

Retribution Unleashed

The Man with the White Handkerchief

Café Mocha

###

Links to Purchase Books

http://lulu.com/spotlight/hmcs1946
http://www.smashwords.com/profile/view/hmcs
http://www.amazon.com/-/e/B003ONO6G4
http://www.amazon.co.uk/-/e/B003ONO6G4

Vivienne Diane Neal

Deception in Plain Sight

Introduction

Alone in her majestic manor, Christine Petté knew something was wrong when she came home to an empty house and found a beautiful small chest on her husband's desk. The wooden box, with its intricate handcrafted patterns and sparkling gems, reminded her of a piece that one would find at an auction house or in a museum.

She never questioned her husband's business affairs, but some strange occurrences got her wondering about him, his business, and his inner circle of friends.

There were bizarre phone calls all hours of the night, secret meetings with individuals she never knew or met and packages delivered to the house by scary looking messengers. Then, someone broke into the house while she and her husband were dining at a restaurant in DUMBO, Brooklyn.

Her husband's office was the only room ransacked. Furnishings, papers, and DVDs were scattered all over the place, but the intruder, as far as she knew, took nothing. Two thousand dollars in cash, a Cartier watch, and gold coins worth over five thousand dollars were in his top desk drawer, all visible to the naked eye.

"Honey, what were they looking for, and how could they have missed those items, which were in plain sight?" she asked, reaching for her cell phone.

As she was getting ready to dial 9-1-1, her husband grabbed the phone out of her hand. "There is no need to call the police. It is Halloween; it was probably some kids playing a practical joke. Instead of adorning the house with raw eggs and toilet paper, they decided to remove the spare key from under the doormat, let themselves in and rummage through my office. Nothing is missing. There is no need to get the police involved."

A spare key under the doormat; this is news to me, Christine thought.

Some neighbors did leave their doors unlocked and would place an extra key under the mat or hide it in a flower bin. There were occasional break-ins, but major crimes rarely occurred on the quiet block.

She decided not to pursue the matter. Her husband's tone, body language, and demeanor made it quite clear.

Leave well enough alone. Let sleeping dogs lie dead.

The kind of business her husband was into might have been the reason for the break-in.

Maybe the prowler thought there were pieces worth stealing.

He owned a shop, which sold second-hand junk. Often he would bring items home to restore before offering them to customers.

Since the Great Depression, the economy was in the pits. At the same time, gentrification was spreading throughout the borough like locusts circling cornfields, and high-end shops and restaurants were replacing mom-pop establishments. If three customers came into her husband's shop, it was considered a good day.

Why someone would come into a home just to poke around and not steal a timepiece, coins, and cash, all worth over eight thousand dollars, did not make any sense to her.

But if Mrs. Petté thought these events were strange, she would soon receive a wake-up call that will send her into a hellish tailspin, leaving her asking: "How could I have missed the deception my husband was exhibiting in plain sight?"

Chapter 1

Awesome Petté was a man without scruples. His primary objective was to get rich fast. If it meant using people and ruining their lives, he couldn't care less. As long as he accomplished his goal, that was all that mattered, notwithstanding the consequences.

His parents were born on the island of Guadeloupe. They immigrated to the United Sates in 1978. In 1980, Mrs. Josephina Petté gave birth to a seven-pound baby boy, a phenomenon for the couple. Years earlier, she suffered several miscarriages. Doctors told her she would never be able to carry a pregnancy full-term. Sticking to her convictions, she was going to have her baby no matter what the specialists said.

What do these doctors really know? Who are they to make that kind of decision? Nothing happens before its time. When that time comes, we will name him or her Awesome Petté.

The family was now living in an old tenement on the Lower East Side of Manhattan. Although Mr. Lupé Petté was an enterprising young man and a loving husband and father, money was extremely tight. After working odd jobs for nearly ten years, he managed to scrape up enough money to purchase a coin-operated Laundromat.

Five years later, the business was pulling in over 1.2 million dollars. During this time, people with money were moving into the neighborhood. Folks were bidding on high-priced brownstones, townhouses, condominiums and co-ops.

The Pettés estimated sales would continue to grow. They would purchase a home of their own and live the American dream as homeowners and successful entrepreneurs.

Since many residential properties in Manhattan were out of the couple's price range, they decided to buy a one family estate in Central Brooklyn. The prior owners wanted to get rid of the eyesore and sold it as is. The asking price was ninety thousand dollars, which was a good deal. Similar homes in trendy Brooklyn Heights and Cobble Hill were going for over four hundred thousand dollars and higher on the island of Manhattan.

When it came to renovating the house, Mr. Petté could not distinguish a jackhammer from a Phillips screwdriver. He enlisted the aid of a home restoration company. It took three years to transform the place.

The four-story, five thousand square feet property was now an enchanting manor, consisting of a two-car garage, five bedrooms with adjoining baths/showers, four marble fireplaces, thirteen-inch ceilings, hardwood floors, and an enclosed landscaped garden.

There was a state of the art kitchen, which a chef would have killed for, an open dining area, a high-tech office, and a beautiful finished basement for meetings and entertaining. The living room with its Waterford crystal chandelier added an elegant ambience to the house.

It did not take long for neighbors to begrudge that impressive estate, but soon the tides would turn. The neighborhood would go through a far-reaching shift and property values would start to soar. If the neighbors were thinking about sprucing up their homes, following the Pettés' lead would not have been the smartest move.

Chapter 2

People who once found Brooklyn to be the place to find reasonably priced houses were witnessing the onslaught of gentrification. Homes, bought on the cheap in the '70s, '80s, and '90s, were now going for over seven figures, pricing out existing renters and prospective homebuyers, except for people like the Baileys.

If you did not know who Mary and James Bailey were, you were probably from another planet or in a state of unconsciousness.

In 1974, the couple met in college while taking a course in ethical business practices. It was never love at first sight.

Money and power drew them together. These two entities outweighed passion and love. After graduating from college with a degree in business administration, Mary Collins and James Bailey announced their engagement.

In 1978, the couple became husband and wife. The bride's parents went all out for their only child. Over five hundred guests attended the extravagant wedding ceremony followed by a reception at an exclusive country club in White Plains, New York.

Mary and James came from old money. Throughout Brooklyn and Westchester County, her kinfolks owned commercial and residential properties that were in the family for four generations.

James was originally from Atlanta, Georgia. His parents owned land, a radio station, a weekly newspaper, and a high society magazine, which had a worldwide circulation of five million readers. After his parents died, he assigned the running of the enterprises to a consortium made up of relatives, investors, and silent partners.

The Baileys' tentacles reached out as far as City Hall. They were active in local politics, raised funds for unknown candidates running for local and state office, sat on several corporate boards and attended a popular church that boasted a following of ten thousand members.

Throughout the '80s and '90s, the couple scooped up dilapidated properties on the cheap and restored them into dazzling estates. Today, those homes are selling anywhere from one to five million dollars.

How the Baileys made their money was questionable. By all accounts, they obtained most of their properties using underhanded tactics. They would assist first time homebuyers to obtain mortgages at higher rates than most banks were offering.

Since many depositories were not lending money to people who had bad credit, no credit or too little income to put a deposit down on a home, desperate individuals would seek out the Baileys.

As soon as people purchased their homes, they had no idea they were not the valid owners but the Baileys were since they held the mortgages. Many never read or understood the terms of the agreement they signed.

The Baileys were also in the refinancing business. Homeowners, who borrowed against their homes to upgrade or pay bills, discovered the couple had placed a lien on their properties. Some owners ended up defaulting on their loans, losing their homes to the Baileys whose net worth was over five hundred million dollars.

In 1982, their daughter was born in a private birthing center in downtown Brooklyn. Rumor had it that an anonymous friend of the family was the biological father. Mr. Bailey was unable to impregnate his wife after years of trying. His sperm counts were in short supply, according to some meddlesome neighbors.

Some went so far to imply, "He was impotent." The chitchat was that the real father donated his sperm, but a few folks insisted, "She and that so-called nameless man conceived that child the old fashioned way by banging each other."

No one knew for sure whether these tales were true or false. The town criers had a tendency to see things that were not there. Others enjoyed making up stories to be the center of attention. Some blabbermouths were downright malicious, because they resented the Baileys' money, power, and influence.

Chapter 3

Someone once said, "Christine Bailey was born with a silver spoon in her mouth, and her gums were budding gold teeth."

The staff at the birthing place thought she was the most adorable infant they had ever seen. Her skin gave off a radiant gleam, and her intense brown eyes with blue rims were captivating. One could not help ogling and pampering her as if she were a goddess. Her parents saw her as an endowment from the gods. "We owe the donor an abundance of gratitude," Mrs. Bailey whispered to her husband.

"I agree," he said, smiling.

The nurse entered the room and asked, "What name should be on the birth certificate?"

"Christine Bailey," the mother replied, smiling at her bundle of joy.

When the birth announcement of Christine Bailey appeared in a community newspaper, readers were aghast. Without a tatter of evidence, people started to spread the word as though it was the gospel truth. "It is official. Pastor Christopher Dune is that baby's daddy." Naming the child Christine was a dead giveaway. It was all the proof most individuals needed.

Two days later, mother and child were home. The baby's bedroom looked more like a palace than an infant's room, decorated with custom-made furnishings and imported add-ons. Even the governess and au pair came from abroad.

Relatives and friends came from all over to partake in the christening of Christine Bailey. The blessed event took place at the church where the Rev. Christopher Dune was head minister. He did not officiate over or attend the baptism. He and his wife were vacationing in Costa Rica.

A few reporters, standing in the back of the church, were mumbling among themselves. "Where the devil is Rev. Dune? You think he would be here to witness this special occasion. After all, we all know he is the father." Yet, no one would print such a statement without seeing a birth certificate, naming the pastor as the father. Since his name was not on the document, it became a mute subject.

After the ceremony, guests attended a private gathering at the couple's duplex in Boerum Hill, Brooklyn. The affair was fit for a head of state. An internationally acclaimed chef catered the fare. An inebriated relative blurted, "This party is more for the adults than it is for the little one."

Nothing was ever too good for their baby girl. The world was her oyster. She wore the finest designer clothes, had shoes for every occasion and enough playthings to open a toy store. Private boarding schools were already bombarding the Baileys with brochures and applications for their child's early enrollment.

Many couples would submit requests to top-quality private schools as soon as the baby popped out of the mother's womb. Christine's parents never had to worry about which school their daughter would attend. They sat on the board and contributed money to an elite private school in Brooklyn Heights. There would always be a spot for their little dumpling.

Parents, who were not on par with the Baileys, were green with envy. "Their daughter is no better than any other child in this community. Who does that family think they are, acting all high and mighty and treating that kid as though she is the princess of Benin?"

Children would yell, "Your daddy is not your daddy, but he knows who is."

Seeing how resentful many of the neighbors and their children were and the harassment their daughter would have to face, her parents decided to ship Christine to a celebrated private primary-secondary school in Atlanta. Her husband's mother and grandmother attended that school, which had a zero tolerance to bullying.

After graduating at the top of her class, Christine remained in Atlanta, went on to a prestigious college, and graduated summa cum laude with a Master's Degree in Business, Marketing, and Finance.

A year later, she returned to Brooklyn and got a job as an instructor, teaching the elements of business at a neighborhood community center.

Being educated, beautiful, and successful, Christine attracted men like moths to flames, but most of these lads were either seeking a one-night stand, a friend with benefits or a sugar momma. Her parents always instilled, "You are a Bailey and with that name comes important responsibilities. Being a young woman of wealth and privilege, your friends should reflect those same qualities."

Most of the affluent men were in committed relationships or married. A few had mistresses on the side, but a woman in Christine's position would never be any man's by side. Her mind would always go back to those words her mother drilled into her head, "Your body is a temple. Once you sleep with a man, he will never respect you. You will forever be seen as a loose woman."

Working at her parents' businesses did not fare any better. Most of the men she encountered were holding down two or more jobs just to make ends meet. The last thing she wanted was to take care of some man who did not have a kettle in which to boil water.

She knew a few female associates who kept men, buying their affection just for the sake of bragging, "I have a man in my life." She wanted no part of this mindset.

A woman should never support a man who is always insolvent, she thought.

Soon, Christine would turn twenty-five and without a husband, not that her parents would ever pressure her to get married. Women in her circle were delaying marriage and not having children until their careers were on track.

Would I ever find Mr. Right before I reach twenty-eight? Christine wondered.

She understood that having it all at once was not plausible. At least she had her degree, a profession, and her trust fund, which she would start to draw from on her 25th birthday.

Christine did not know it then, but her luck was about to change. A man, whom she believes is the one, will fuel her to the point of no return. All of the advice her mother gave her about men would go straight out the window.

Chapter 4

Awesome Petté and Christine Bailey were destined to meet. Both of their families were successful. Although, her family was more prosperous than his was. His family could not hold a candle in their world. Old money carried more standing than some Johnny-come-lately, which was what the Pettés were, arriving too late to the billionaires' ball.

The community center, where Christine worked, provided preparation and assistance to people who wanted to start their own venture or make improvements on an existing business. Volunteering her expertise in this area was one way to give back to the community.

Her parents would say, "It is your duty to help those who are less fortunate than you are." Whether it was out of guilt for having so much given to her or just being altruistic, Christine would become a non-paying consultant to potential or current entrepreneurs at the center.

When she first walked into the classroom, a feeling of ecstasy took control of her body. She could not comprehend why these emotions were starting to overpower her. She was never one to allow anything or anyone to distract her from her work.

What is going on here? What is happening to me? My panties are moist; my nipples are hard. I had better start meditating before I end up embarrassing myself. Finally, those feel-good sensations subsided.

Scanning the room, she took a deep breath and introduced herself. "Good morning, ladies and gentlemen. My name is Ms. Christine Bailey, but you may call me Christine." She had to pause for a second. "I will be your instructor for the next twelve weeks. Before we begin, tell me why you are here; what do you hope to get out of this course, and what are your plans for the future."

There were eight students taking the course. Each person gave some information about him or herself.

"I would like to open a daycare center."

"My intention is to start a tech company."

"Opening a clothing store has always been a dream of mine."

"We can always use more eating establishments in our community."

"I am very good at styling hair. My goal is to open a hair salon."

Suddenly, a voice interjected, "Hello, Christine. My name is Awesome Petté. I am taking this course because I plan to become a millionaire before age thirty."

Christine was in a state of amusement. "Mr. Petté, are you trying to be funny? Did someone say you were awesome, and you could not take a joke?" Everyone roared with laughter.

"No! I am not attempting to be a comedian. My first name is Awesome. If you check your roster, you will see. My parents bestowed that name to me for reasons I do not wish to discuss. Perhaps, over dinner, I can tell you why they gave me that name," he responded, gazing at her vertically.

By now, some of the students were beginning to dislike his attitude and saw him as an arrogant little man and a butt kisser. If Christine had those same thoughts, no one in the classroom would ever know, because Awesome Petté had her completely under his control.

She now understood why those hidden sentiments exploded inside of her when she walked into that classroom. *That fine-looking hunk was transmitting telepathic vibrations to me. Lord, deliver me from temptation.*

While talking, Christine had trouble concentrating. She was fumbling over her words. At times, she was repeating herself. Students were beginning to notice her eyeballs fixated on Awesome. It was as though no one else was in that room but the two of them.

The class was supposed to meet for two hours, but Christine decided to end the lecture after sixty minutes. Everyone got the message: Awesome Petté was going to be her little pet.

Chapter 5

Awesome Petté was a slippery character. He recognized Christine was attracted to him, and he would use that infatuation to ingratiate himself into her world. He had an advantage over the rest of the students because he was the only one whose parents owned a business.

When it came to his homework assignments, he was always on top of his game, challenging the instructor and guest speakers on the subjects of business, finance, and marketing. With his PowerPoint slides, he showed growth patterns and profits from his parents' Laundromat. It got to the point where Awesome became the whiz kid, and Christine became the passive coach.

By the tenth week, the class dwindled to three students. Christine could now devote more time to each pupil, which was right up Awesome's alley. He was now ready to move in for the kill.

Rather than have a graduation ceremony and party with just three people, Christine arranged to take the graduates to a Caribbean restaurant, which was not too far from the center.

She arrived at the restaurant first. Fifteen minutes later, Awesome walked in and was carrying a bouquet of red roses. The other two graduates never showed.

"Again, it is a pleasure to see you, Christine. These flowers are for you."

"Thank you, Awesome. These are beautiful. That was so thoughtful of you."

"I go all out for such an exquisite lady." Instantly, his charisma was turning her on.

The waiter came over. "Good evening, would you like to order a drink?"

"I'll take a margarita," Christine replied.

"For me, a manhattan," he said to the waiter. "Christine, this is a nice place. How did you hear about this spot?"

"My parents own this building and are silent partners in the restaurant, which opened in 1990. Even though more upscale restaurants are opening, this place is remarkably sound. People come from all over to taste authentic West Indian food."

"Oh, that is very interesting," Awesome said.

She went on to say, "Other businesses were not so lucky. Property owners were raising rents anywhere from 100 to 600 percent, which forced many small establishments to close their doors."

If anyone understood how important it was to own a building that houses a business, it was Awesome. Two days ago, he discovered his parents were losing their Laundromat due to eminent domain, the right to take private property for public use. They did not own the building, but if they had, they would have gotten a reasonable compensation.

"Christine, since we are talking about business, I am planning to open a shop called *Second Hand Treasures*, selling refurbished furniture and other knickknacks and have just put together a business plan and loan proposal. I would appreciate it if you could look it over and provide me with your feedback."

"That sounds wonderful. I would be delighted to look over your proposal and give you some pointers." She started to read. "I love the name of your business. It is very catchy.

But before I forget, why did your parents name you Awesome?"

"My mother had several miscarriages before she had me. Doctors told her she would never carry a pregnancy full-term. Of course, she did not pay any attention to them and kept trying. Finally, I came into the world in 1980. Whether I was a boy or a girl, they were going to name me Awesome, their miracle *bébé*, which is French for baby."

"Were your parents born in France?"

"No. They are from Guadeloupe and came to America, the land of opportunity, in 1978."

The waiter returned with their drinks. "Would you like to order now or need more time?"

"We will order now," Awesome said.

Christine liked the idea that he was a take-charge man with a good business sense and saw herself spending the rest of her life with him. He saw her as his cash cow.

Chapter 6

After losing their business, Awesome's parents became disillusioned. "Son, we have decided to go back to Guadeloupe and will leave you in charge of the house."

He was delighted to hear such news. "Papa, I will make you proud of me. I have great plans for this place. When are you leaving?"

"Your mother and I will be leaving next Friday morning and will purchase our tickets at LaGuardia Airport. We are not taking any furniture or appliances with us and will be staying with friends until we find a place of our own."

Awesome could not go with his parents to the airport that morning because he had a prior appointment, which he could not change. On his way out, he hugged them and wished them a safe trip. "Call me when you land," he said, grinning like a Cheshire cat.

"Son, we will let you know what our plans are after we arrive on the island. Be good and take care of yourself."

When it came to the Laundromat, Awesome was never interested in taking over the business. Consequently, its closing was a blessing. To purchase commercial space for his shop, he would refinance the house and use the money to buy a two-story commercial building with retail space.

He knew people who had money, but it was never quite clear if they would invest in his venture. The loan he would get on his home would not be sufficient. If he could not get the financing he needed, he had a backup plan.

One month later, Awesome received a letter from *Home Financial Services*, the company holding the mortgage:

August 30, 2007

Dear Lupé/Josephina Petté:

We are writing to inform you that you are six months behind on your mortgage payments. If you are having a financial hardship, we can modify your loan to make it more affordable.

We do not want you to lose your house. Making a few payments will prevent a foreclosure. We are giving you ninety days to submit full or partial payments.

If you have any questions or need additional assistance, please do not hesitate to contact us. I remain,

Very truly yours,

Benjamin Anderson
Loan Modification Specialist
Home Financial Services

What his parents neglected to tell him was that the house was heavily into debt. They took profits from the Laundromat to pay for the renovation and upkeep of their home, not realizing the huge expense it would take to maintain that mansion and the high taxes they would have to pay each year, so they refinanced the property. *Home Financial Services* owns the property until someone pays the loan in full.

He was about to call his parents in Guadeloupe but remembered they never gave him any contact information. He never met or heard about any of his other relatives; as a result, he could not contact them.

After coming to New York, my mom and dad never went back to that island for a visit or vacation, he thought.

Awesome recognized that he knew nothing about his family tree. All he knew was that his parents arrived in New York in 1978. He was born in 1980. Whether his parents became USA citizens, he did not know.

He was not sure where his parents kept all of their papers, deeds, and other pertinent documents. When he went into their bedroom to check, he could not find anything. He searched all of the other rooms, including the office, but he found nothing.

Immediately, he called Christine and explained his predicament. "I need your help. My parents are behind on their mortgage payments." After explaining the situation to her, she agreed to come to his place the following evening.

How could they leave me holding the bag? Awesome could not understand how his parents fell into this abyss. *This is probably why they got out of town and took all of the documents with them.*

Yet, he would not be alone facing financial difficulties. The increase in subprime mortgage lending will set off a firestorm, leading to delinquencies and foreclosures. The stock market will tank. Some regional banks will fail. Many people will lose their jobs. The country will be at its worst downturn since the Great Depression.

Not everyone will be crying poormouth. A few will make out like gangbusters, and Awesome will make certain he gets his hefty piece of that pie.

Chapter 7

If the Baileys did not like you, you had two enemies for life. When they did not get their way, someone would suffer the consequences from their wrath. Once you went back on your word, you became the focus of humiliation. Many folks feared them and a few kissed up to them just to be in their good graces.

An elected official found that out the hard way. The Baileys asked him to make certain their bid to procure an entertainment complex in Jamaica, Queens would be a done deal. "You have my word. I would not be where I am today if it were not for you and your husband's support," the official said.

However, the deal fell through. Another buyer with more money and influence and the promise to finance the district leader's reelection outweighed what the Baileys were offering.

A month later, the elected official resigned amid a blaze of disgrace. His extramarital affair with his boy toy was front-page news. The lover lived in a townhouse that was paid for by the taxpayers and with campaign money. Six months later, his wife divorced him and received a five million dollar settlement. She got custody of their three children, the house, where the debauchery took place, and the summer home in the Hamptons.

If the Baileys' daughter selected a beau who did not measure up to their standards, he would never become a permanent fixture in that dynasty. Dating or marrying a commoner would only happen over their dead bodies.

While Christine was attending college, she was seeing a young man. His name was Henry Fuller. His father was a janitor at an elementary school, and his mother worked at a fast-food restaurant. Henry was a stock clerk at an upscale clothing store in downtown Atlanta.

Their relationship was strictly platonic but word got back to her parents, who had their own views as to the type of man their daughter should be seeing.

Christine's mother knew people in high and low places. She made a call. "Hello, Razor, this is Mary."

"What can I do for you, Ma'am?"

"A man named Henry Fuller is employed at *Elegant Clothing Store*. I understand the owners keep their receipts in a cigar box. I want you to find someone to break into that store, steal the box with the money and place it into Henry's residence. Here is his address. You will be paid handsomely."

"No problem, Mrs. Bailey. I am familiar with the shop. Consider it done."

After closing hours, a professional thief entered the store, went straight to the office, checked to make certain the money was there and grabbed the box.

The robber then drove to the building where Henry lived, entered the dwelling and found his way into the bedroom. Henry was sound asleep. The intruder planted the cash under the bed and left through the front door; he placed the chain back into the lock with a special gizmo, got into his car and drove off like a bat out of hell.

The next day, the proprietors discovered the money was gone. There was a message on the answering machine: "You will find the stolen money under Henry Fuller's bed." The owner quickly called the police.

When the officers arrived, they listened to the recording. "Does Mr. Fuller have a key to your store or access to your office?" one of the officers asked.

"No! My wife and I are the only people with keys, and the office is always locked when the store is closed."

"How many people do you employ?"

"Presently, Mr. Fuller is the only employee. We just hired two salespersons due to start work next Monday."

"Since there are no signs of forced entry, we will question Mr. Fuller. Will he be coming in today?"

"No. He is off today."

Henry was preparing breakfast when he heard a pounding at the door. When he responded, he was befuddled to see two officers standing there. "Are you Mr. Henry Fuller?" The police never let on that someone had accused him of stealing money.

"Yes, sir, I am. What can I do for you?"

"We are sorry to disturb you. Last night, someone broke into the store where you work and stole a box containing cash. May we come in and look around?"

With a nervous twitch, Henry answered, "No problem, I have nothing to hide. I would never steal from my bosses. Mr. and Mrs. Clark have been very kind to me." When the two officers went into his bedroom and looked under the bed, they found the cigar box containing $3500.

"I never stole that money and do not know how it got there," he said, shaking and crying. The police read him his *Miranda* rights and arrested him.

Since the owners got all of their money back, they refused to press charges. The couple could not fathom why Henry would steal the money. "He has been with us for two years and never showed any signs of financial hardship. If he needed money, we would have gladly assisted him."

Convincing the owners and the police that he did not take the money was futile. As far as anyone was concerned, Henry stole the money. A man in his position did not have the means to hire a PI to probe and find the real culprit. To avoid any further shame, he decided to put the incident behind him.

Even though the police did not charge him with any wrongdoing, Henry understood the problems he would face trying to find work. This kind of news could never remain hidden. Discussions about the theft were beginning to circulate around town faster than a tornado.

Mrs. Bailey received a call. "Henry Fuller is yesterday's news."

"Thank you. I have wired ten thousand dollars into your offshore account."

Christine never knew what her mother had done. When she discovered Henry had left town without saying a word, people would only say, "He bit off the hand that fed him."

If Mary and James thought they were in control of everything, the couple was mistaken. Their money, power, and influence will not mean diddly squat because someone is planning to release their brand of clout, which will result in scandal, mayhem and the obliteration of the Baileys' empire.

Chapter 8

Christine had a 6 p.m. appointment with Awesome. She was trying to figure out what to wear. In her large closet were top designer clothes; it would take her hours to select the proper attire.

This is a business meeting. Therefore, I must dress the part, she thought.

Even though she was engrossed with Awesome, showing up in a sexy outfit would be a deal breaker.

Not only would he not take me seriously, but he may also see me as nothing more than a tramp hankering for sex.

She selected a red suit, yellow pumps, and a brown clutch bag. Coordinating colors was never one of her strong suits.

During spring and summer breaks, she would often see her parents wear neutral colors when they met with business associates.

Her mother, a fashion connoisseur, would say, "Colors should always be synchronized." Christine would see people wearing bold and mismatched colors, especially in the summer. Her mother would refer to these hues as "uncanny motifs, loud and drawing a crowd." She would laugh at her mother's comments, which were sometimes spiteful jabs at people who were not part of the upper echelon.

Awesome could not find the deed to the house and concluded that he would probably never hear from his parents. He would ask Webster Jones, his best friend, to create one.

When it came to phony credentials, Webster was a pro extraordinaire. Whatever documents a person needed, he or she got it. As long as you had the dough, you were in like Flint. His work was flawless, could fool the most seasoned authority and pass through any scanning device without triggering an alarm.

Awesome and Webster met in high school, instantly became friends and were two peas in a pod. They were the modern-day *Butch Cassidy and the Sundance Kid*. Learning was never part of their agenda, but getting over was. When it came to manipulating people, they were masters in disguise.

If they chose to, they could have easily played on the football or basketball team. The two were tall, dark, and handsome, well endowed, and knew how to use their physical attributes to entice female students to be at their beck and call.

Desperate females would do just about anything to get Awesome and Webster's attention. A few would do the boys' homework, read books assigned by their teachers, and write glowing book reports. The two breezed through high school without ever breaking a sweat.

The school was conducting a writing contest for seniors. *Where Do I See Myself in Ten Years* was the theme. The first prize was $10,000, the second prize was $5,000, and the third prize was $2,500. Winners would also have their work published in an educational magazine distributed to high schools and colleges throughout the United States and its territories.

Awesome and Webster wanted to enter that contest. The first person who came to mind was another senior named Beatrice Moon. She was the smartest student in the school but not too fortunate when it came to attracting boys. Many would say, "She has the face only a mother could love."

She had the hots for Awesome and Webster. Had they asked her to, she would have walked barefooted on hot coal, thinking it was the best approach to losing her virginity. They implored her to create unique narratives for them, and she was more than happy to oblige.

Beatrice felt like the luckiest girl in school to be so close to Awesome and Webster, which in her mind was better than sex. Never expecting anything in return for her service, she submitted the writings to the judging panel.

Thinking that both of them would be grateful for what she did, Beatrice asked Awesome to take her to the senior prom. "Sorry, but I am taking someone else," he quickly replied.

She then asked Webster, who politely whispered, "I will be out of town that day."

One afternoon, Beatrice overheard the two talking about her.

Awesome: "I would have to be an owl to take that ugly duckling to the prom."

Webster: "If I ever went to bed with her, I would insist she put a paper bag over her head. I would gag trying to kiss those horse lips."

After hearing those comments, she started to cry.

How could I have been so stupid, thinking those guys actually liked me? Beatrice thought.

At the graduation ceremony, the principal announced the winners of the writing contest. To add more insult to injury, Awesome won first prize, and Webster won second prize. "We did it," they said, hugging and doing the high-five to each other but never acknowledging or thanking the one who was solely responsible for their victory.

Sitting in the audience was a fuming Beatrice, visualizing what she would do to those two characters for their deceitfulness. *If I had the power, I would send Awesome and Webster straight to hell.*

Webster got a job at a printing company, where he learned all the ins and outs designing brochures and flyers for small, medium, and large companies.

After ten years on the job, he left and started his own illegal enterprise, making fake ID cards and documents. His goal was to make quick and easy cash and travel the world. "There is money to be made designing counterfeit papers," he would tell Awesome, who was now working full-time at his parents' Laundromat.

"If I ever need your service, I will give you a call," Awesome said, bantering.

Chapter 9

The doorbell rang. As always, Christine was on time. She learned early on that time is money and went back to the story her father once told her.

A venture capitalist had one million dollars to invest into a start-up company. Two people were vying for that money. The first person had a 10 a.m. appointment. The second one had an 11 a.m. meeting.

The 10 a.m. appointment arrived one hour early. The capitalist said, "You have a good business plan but it needs a lot of tweaking. I will contact you with my decision."

The 11 a.m. appointment arrived at 12 noon. Without meeting with that person or reading his business proposal, the capitalist said, "Thank you for coming, but I have decided to invest my money with someone else who was courteous enough to show up on time."

Christine understood what her father was trying to convey. *It is better to be one hour early than one minute late. Punctuality is a sign of respect.*

Awesome was planning to order take-out. Cooking was women's work. He could not melt butter if his life depended on it. His mother was the cook, and that kitchen was her domain. She once stated, "The way to a man's heart is through his stomach."

That can also work for a woman's heart, but someone else will have to do the cooking, he thought.

He remembered how his mother would devote so much time caring for the home, shopping, and preparing and cooking for the family. As much time as she spent working with his dad at the Laundromat, she always found the vigor to keep a spotless home, cook scrumptious meals and put together a table setting that was worthy of a blue ribbon award.

Although his parents came over as having money, he now realized it was a pipedream. He assumed wealthy people had servants to perform such household tasks, and his mom and dad should have had that luxury.

He wore a gray pinstriped suit, a light blue shirt and a dark blue tie. He looked into the mirror and could not help gloating. *I will have that chick eating out of my hand.*

Awesome dashed down the stairs and opened the door. Seeing her, he almost had an erection. "Christine, it is so nice to see you. You look amazing."

"Thank you. You look like a million dollar executive," she said.

"Please, allow me." He took her hand, kissed it and escorted her into the living room.

She started to feel horny, but the chandelier distracted her. "Is that a Waterford?"

"Yes, it is. You know your chandeliers."

"Several of my parents' properties have them. They add such grace to a room and are great selling points."

"Christine, why don't you make yourself at home? May I offer you a drink?"

"Not at the moment. When conducting business, I like to keep a clear head."

"I am ordering take-out. As I recall, your favorite is chicken and rice."

"How sweet of you to remember."

"I take great pride in knowing the likes and dislikes of the woman I plan to marry." She looked at him as though he were an alien from another planet. He saw the shocking look on her face and quickly said, "I am just playing with you." She did not realize then, but his remarks were a self-fulfilling prophecy.

The dinner arrived: Fried chicken, yellow rice, fried plantains, and bok choy sautéed in lime sauce. They would eat first and discuss business afterward.

"Awesome, this is delicious. I will need the name of the restaurant that put together this delightful meal."

"It is *Joe's Chicken Joint*, which is two blocks from here. They serve a variety of chicken dishes."

After finishing their meal, the two went into the office.

"Christine, I have a dilemma. Here is the letter I received. Unfortunately, I do not know where my parents are and have not heard from them since they left over a month ago. They left me in charge of the house but never told me they took out a second mortgage."

She read the letter and knew the company, which had a pristine reputation.

"When your parents first bought the house, did they borrow the money from a bank?"

"No. They paid cash for the house."

"I see. Are you their only child?"

"Yes."

"And your parents went back to Guadeloupe?"

"That's correct."

"Then it should not be difficult to find them. I have an associate who is good at finding people. Give me a couple of days, and I will get back to you regarding this matter."

"Christine, I am beholden to you."

"Awesome, I got a chance to study your business plan, which by the way is superb. With so many wealthy people buying and upgrading homes, you should have no problems reaching these prospective customers. I know you want to refinance this house, but you do not want to add on more debt. You will have to pay off the loan and then have the house transferred into your name, but you will not be able to do this until your parents are found."

"Yes, people are always throwing away good stuff and do not realize the true value of those items. I am good at restoring old furniture, so that is a plus for me. It is something I learned from my father."

"You are a man of many talents."

"Christine, you have given me a lot to chew on. I know people with money, but whether they would be willing to lend me the capital I need, I don't know."

"Awesome, do not worry about the money. We will cross that bridge when we come to it."

"It is time to take a break from talking business and money. Let me give you a tour of the house."

The mansion overwhelmed Christine. She could not remember ever seeing such a stupendous estate and thought her parents were the epitome of style when it came to converting dumps into million-dollar showpieces.

His parents must have spent gazillions of dollars renovating and maintaining this home, she thought.

Since there were no records or receipts to check, she was taking an educated guess as to how much his parents were spending on this place.

"How do you like it so far?" he asked.

"It is out of this world. I would buy this place in a heartbeat."

"How much do you think it is worth?"

"Houses of this caliber are going for over two million dollars."

"I do not want to lose this house; my parents put their heart and soul into buying and fixing this place. It would be heartbreaking to lose it," he said, pretending to be sad.

"Awesome, do not worry. You will not lose this house. I will not let that happen." She grabbed and squeezed his hand. He knew then that his plans were about to fall into place.

Chapter 10

As she promised, Christine contacted an associate whose specialty was locating people. No matter where they were, or how much they wanted to remain under the radar, he could find them.

A relentless tracker, he could unearth just about anything: a hidden offshore account, a long lost relative, a recipient to a large inheritance. He did not come cheap. Whatever his asking price was, he was worth every penny. His name was Danny Mayo.

Danny was a longtime associate of the Baileys and performed unusual jobs for the couple. To say he was a sleaze was an understatement. He was always one-step ahead of the law when it came to conducting crooked deals. People who did not want to get their hands dirty would hire him. As long as he got the job done, and his unauthorized activities did not come back to bite those folks in the behind, he was good enough for them

As he was about to leave his office, the phone rang. The answering machine kicked in. "This is Christine Bailey. I..." When he heard who it was, he quickly picked up the receiver.

"Hello, Christine, I was just on my way out. It is so nice hearing from you. It has been a long time. How are you?"

"I am fine, Mr. Mayo, and thank you for asking."

"What can I do for you?"

"The reason why I am calling is that I have a job for you. I need you to find my client's parents; they went back home to Guadeloupe, and he has not heard from them since, does not have contact information and needs to get in touch with them."

"I will need their names, the airport where they flew from, the day they left, and the flight number."

"There is a problem. I can only give you their names, which are Lupé and Josephina Petté. They took off from LaGuardia airport on Friday, July 27."

"You have given me enough to go on. I will get back to you in a day or two."

"Please, bill me, and do not mention this to my parents. This is between you and me."

"I understand. The information I collect is strictly for you. Confidentiality is my number one priority."

"Thank you, Mr. Mayo. It was a pleasure talking to you."

"It was nice hearing from you too."

Danny was in the business long enough to guess that the Pettés were probably on the run. Why else would they leave and not provide pertinent information on how their son could reach them. His job was not to figure out why they left but to get an address or phone number and pass it on to his client.

To Danny's surprise, Lupé and Josephina Petté did not fly from LaGuardia to Guadeloupe. He checked the whole month of July, and no couple by that name was on the passenger or flight manifest.

He then went on the Internet, did a search but had no luck. Finally, he sent an electronic message to his friend, George, who was a law enforcement agent on that island, requesting the whereabouts of the couple. If anyone knew anything, it would be him.

Two days later, Danny received a reply: *There is no record of a Lupé or Josephina Petté ever living on this island.*

Danny called Christine and gave her his findings. For his work, he charged her one hundred and fifty dollars. She went to his office and paid him in cash. "Sorry, I could not be of more help. This is the first time a case has stumped me. This will go down in history."

"Don't lose sleep over it. Your reputation will continue to precede you," she said, leaving the office in a perplexed state.

Chapter 11

Awesome and Webster met at a local bar in the Bronx, where Webster lived, to discuss their next move.

"Christine loved my business plan and found the house irresistible. It will not be long before I have her writing a check to me," Awesome said.

"Man, you sure know how to pick them. She will be giving it up in no time, if you know what I mean," Webster said, laughing so hard that his drink almost went down the wrong windpipe.

"I told her I did not want to lose the house. She said, 'Not to worry.'"

"So, what's next?"

"Hopefully, she will contact me soon regarding the location of my parents. I will be able to get them to sign a document, giving me title to the house, and we will take it from there."

"Sounds like a good plan," Webster said.

Awesome's cell phone was vibrating. "Webster, there's a call coming in."

It was Christine with bad news. "My contact checked all the flights leaving from LaGuardia during the month of July. There is no record of your parents flying to that island. He was also told they never lived in Guadeloupe."

"What! There must be some mistake. They were born on that island; that's what they told me!"

"Since you cannot find any documents proving this, you should contact a lawyer, or I can recommend one," she suggested.

"I will use my parents' attorney, but he is away on business and will not be back until next month. After I talk to him, I will call you," he said. Without saying another word, he hung up on her.

"Webster, you are not going to believe what just happened. According to Christine's contact, my parents did not go to Guadeloupe and were never born there."

"Are you pulling my leg?" Webster asked with a dumbfounded expression.

"No! I am serious. This changes everything. We must regroup and come up with another ploy."

The two had to put their heads together. Getting that house in Awesome's name was going to take some maneuvering. Webster came up with a brilliant idea. "If you do not hear from your mom and dad, I know this couple who can pretend to be your parents, and I can produce all the papers and affidavits that will help you get that house into your name."

Awesome was listening and jotting down notes. "I will need a lawyer who is willing to sell his soul to Lucifer to represent me. I will not use Christine's attorney."

"I know just the person. Give me one week to get all the players together and to find out what forms you will need to transfer the house into your name."

"Good, let us order another drink," Awesome said in a confident tone.

The couple, who Webster mentioned, agreed to participate in the hoax. They would pretend to be Lupé and Josephina Petté. It would take him several days to come up with a bogus marriage license, social security cards, immigration papers and a deed to the house. Since Awesome could not find his birth certificate, Webster would make one for him.

One week later, Awesome received his birth certificate, an affidavit that would give him ownership of the house, other various papers and a quitclaim deed form. Webster charged five thousand dollars for his work, which covered the hiring of the couple, research, supplies, printing and other miscellaneous expenditures.

With a convincing story, Awesome was ready to play the most diabolical role of his life. He called Christine and said, "I have good news. Let us get together tomorrow evening at *Joe's Chicken Joint*. It will be my treat. How does 6:30 p.m. sound?"

"That is fine, but I rather have dinner at your place, which is more serene. I can stop at *Joe's Chicken Joint*. What would you like?" she asked.

"Surprise me."

Christine did not see her meeting with Awesome as strictly business and chose to wear a sexy outfit, not too revealing but just enough to leave something to the imagination.

A red bustier, black leggings and red and black stilettos should do the trick, she thought. Because her skin was flawless, she never had to wear makeup. *Tonight, I am going to let my hair down.*

When the doorbell rang, Awesome was on the phone with Webster. "That must be her. I will call you tomorrow to let you know how the evening went. Wish me luck."

"You will do just fine."

When he opened the door, Christine could have knocked him over with a feather. For the first time in his life, he was speechless. "It is so nice to see you," she said, embracing him as though she had not seen him for eons.

"Likewise," he mumbled. For one second, he thought he had died and gone to paradise erotica. Promptly, he got a hold of himself. He took her into the dining room; paper plates, plastic knives, and forks were on the table.

"Awesome, I ordered smothered chicken, wild rice, and kale. Hope you like it."

"What's not to like. The food smells good and looks luscious," he said.

Just like you, she thought.

They each said grace and then started to chomp down on the food. "Yummy. This is my first time eating smothered chicken. My mother would bake, fry, or grill the bird," Awesome said, biting into that fowl, as though it was his last meal.

"I am delighted you like it. Now, I know how you like your chicken. When I cook for you, I will also prepare it the way your mother does."

"Speaking of my mother, I finally heard from her and my father. They apologized for taking so long to get back to me."

"When did you hear from them?"

"It was about a week ago. They were not aware that they were behind on their mortgage payments. After losing the Laundromat, they became inundated with obligations and decided to leave."

"Did they explain why they said they were born in Guadeloupe?"

"My parents were actually born in Martinique. They left that island to work for a wealthy family in Guadeloupe but never used their real names. There was no record of them ever arriving or working in Guadeloupe. You could say they were undocumented, worked off the books and saved enough money to come to America. This is why your friend could not find them on that island."

"Hearing from your parents must have been a relief."

"It was. I thought something had happened to them. Anyway, I explained the situation to them; by special delivery, they will send me everything that I will need to transfer the house into my name, but they don't have the money to pay off the loan."

"I am glad everything worked out for you, Awesome, but do not worry about paying off the loan. We will work something out."

"I am too. Christine, this must remain between us. I do not want to get my parents into any trouble."

"I do understand. Your secret is safe with me."

Smiling, he opened a bottle of wine, poured it into his and her glass and said, "To a happy, beautiful, and successful future."

Chapter 12

Mary and James Bailey were planning an open house for a townhouse they bought on the cheap several years ago in Fort Greene, Brooklyn. It was an enormous four-story residence on a historic block.

Registered as a two family estate, the duplex offered original details, six bedrooms with six marble baths, a gourmet kitchen, an enormous living room, four wood-burning fireplaces, a rooftop garden, and a finished basement. The opening bid was 2 million dollars.

Christine would serve as the host and tour guide. She would also take care of advertising and promoting the event in an upscale weekly.

While discussing the details with her parents, her cell phone rang. It was Awesome. "Guess what? I received all of the documents from my parents. If we could meet, at your convenience, I would like to discuss my next step. This is all new to me."

"Have you spoken to your parents' lawyer?"

"No, since I have never had any dealings with him, I thought I would talk to you first, listen to what he has to say and make certain he is on the up and up."

"That makes good sense. Can I call you back? I am in the middle of an important meeting."

"I will be home all day."

"Good, I will call you back this afternoon."

While Awesome was on the phone with Christine, Webster and Boris Winston were sitting in the garden going over their roles to play.

Boris was an amoral lawyer. He would take short cuts for the right fee. He did not see any problems with the fake documents passing as valid credentials. Besides, he did take some acting classes. His claim to fame was appearing as an extra on a TV crime drama, which never aired.

"I just got off the phone with Christine. She is at a meeting and will call me back."

"Did she tell you what the meeting is about?" Webster asked.

"No, but I am sure she will. After all, she is falling for me. It will not be long before we get hitched."

"If you need an officiant to perform the ceremony, I'm your man," Boris said. All three laughed and went back to rehearsing their roles.

It was after two when Christine called. "Hi, Awesome, would it be okay if I come over now? I could be there in thirty minutes."

"Sure, come on over."

"Have you eaten?" she asked.

"Yes, I had some leftovers from last night."

"Fine, I will bring dessert."

"You guys will have to leave. Christine is on her way." Webster and Boris left and wished him the best of luck.

Awesome went to take a quick shower. He wanted to be spanking fresh and ready.

I will bring dessert. What did she mean by that statement?

He went back to the night when Christine was dress like a woman of the night, but he held back and did not want to come over as though he were a tomcat in heat. The last thing he wanted to do was to chase her away. He would let her make the first move and win her over by being the perfect gent.

Awesome had known her for six months. Most relationship experts say, "Wait at least ninety days before engaging in sex."

Heck, I have waited one hundred and eighty days, which is a long time for me. It is time for me to work my mojo on her.

Chapter 13

Christine arrived at 5:30 p.m. She was wearing a winter green silk dress. Awesome had on jeans and a black T-shirt. She kissed him on the cheek. He returned the gesture.

"Let us go into the garden. What type of dessert did you bring?"

"It's a surprise. I think you will enjoy it."

He noticed that she was not carrying anything in her hand, and her purse was too small to hold the kitchen sink much less something sweet.

"You have a beautiful garden. How do you maintain it?" she asked.

"My parents have a landscaping service coming in. The contract does not run out until the end of the year. Unless my finances improve, I may not be able to continue using the service."

"Awesome, you must stop being a worrywart."

On the bench were the documents for Christine to check. She read them. "Everything seems to be in order. You have the deed with both your parents' names. I see they both signed the quitclaim deed transferring home ownership to you. Now you must have the form notarized."

"Okay, I know a notary public and will take it to him on Monday."

"No need to go to him. I can notarize it."

"Christine, you are full of revelations. Who knew you were a notary public."

"It is something that I have been doing for quite some time." She took the stamp out of her bag and notarized the form.

"You are a lifesaver. Thank you."

With her tempting eyes, she said, "I am always happy to help a future entrepreneur."

"What do I do next?"

"You must file the quitclaim form with the county office where the original deed is recorded. Remember to ask for a certified copy of the quitclaim deed when you file it. You may have to pay a small fee for this, but it can assist you if the filing ever comes into question. Make certain you keep a copy in a safe place."

"I will check with the lawyer to see if he provides me with the same or additional information. He is due back next week."

"This is good because you will need to retain a good lawyer when you become the sole owner of this house and launch your business."

This woman sure knows her stuff, he thought.

"Enough about business. It is time for that dessert you promised me," he said, salivating.

Christine was getting hotter by the second; getting up, she took Awesome's hand, pressed her body against his and placed her tongue into his mouth. Feeling his hand moving slowly up her legs, she sensed someone was watching them. It was the next-door neighbor with binoculars. *A Peeping Tom,* she thought.

Being somewhat bashful, she whispered, "Someone is watching us. Let's go inside." Awesome picked her up, took her indoors, and carried her up the stairs and into his boudoir.

They slowly undressed each other. He positioned her on the bed; with his fingers, he started to stimulate her swollen and soaked labia. She screamed, "Oh my goodness!" When she saw his erect organ, she could not believe how humongous it was. He then deposited his branch inside of her. Her G-spot sprung into uninterrupted bliss. The lovemaking lasted until midnight.

When Christine and Awesome woke up, it was 9 a.m. She was still experiencing orgasms and wanted to continue her rumble in the bed with him. "Honey, let's do it again," she pleaded, touching his blade. He was pooped and could not believe how energized she was after last night's actions.

He tried to resist her but surrendered; this time, she was the dominant one, demanding she be on top. She was pretending to be a cowgirl and riding him as though he were a stallion. "Giddy up, giddy up," she shouted. With her tantalizing and thrusting moves, she brought herself intense gratification. "Your parents gave you the correct name. When it comes to lovemaking, you are awesome." After making that comment, she realized he had fallen asleep.

She got out of bed and took a shower. After drying herself, she dressed, went downstairs and into the kitchen. The refrigerator was empty but there was instant coffee in the cupboard. She remembered Awesome was not a breakfast person, so she made a cup of coffee for herself.

Her cell phone was buzzing. When she answered, the voice on the other end asked, "Where are you? We are waiting for you to go over the advertisement for the open house." It was 10 a.m. She was supposed to meet with the newspaper editor and her parents at 9:00 a.m.

Forgetting an important conference was something Christine would never overlook. She had to come up with a plausible reason as to why she was not there. "Please, forgive me and extend my apologies to the editor. I had another engagement and did not realize what time it was. I will be there in fifteen minutes."

Awesome was already up. He came downstairs. Christine went to him and said, "Baby, I have to leave and will call you this evening." She kissed him, dashed out of the house, got into her car, and took off like a speeding bullet.

I wonder where she is off to in such a rush. That woman is a bombshell. She comes over as Miss Prim and Proper, but she is an untamed tigress in the bedroom.

He called Webster and gave him all the details about his meeting and Christine's salacious sexual escapades. "I knew you would get lucky," Webster said, cheering Awesome on.

"She fell hook, line, and sinker with the papers and even notarized the quitclaim deed. I will file the form with the court, and the house will be mine."

"And she rewarded you with good sex, or was it the other way around," Webster asked.

"Listen, it was way beyond good; it was out of this world. She wore me out. I fell asleep during the second round."

"What!"

"That's right. She is a pistol-whipping sexpot behind locked doors."

"Well, I guess you have her right where you want her."

"You bet I do. The next phase is to get her to get me that money to prevent the house from going into foreclosure and to invest into my new business. So, I am going to let you go and will talk to you in a couple of days."

"You take care, Awesome."

Chapter 14

As Christine promised, she arrived at the office in fifteen minutes. Her parents and the editor were discussing the placement of the ad for the open house. "Good morning, I apologize for being late."

"No problem," the editor said. "We have decided to run a full-page ad. Here is a proof copy as to what the ad will look like."

"This looks fabulous, and the photo of the exterior and interior of the house is exquisite. The phones will be ringing off the hook when prospective buyers see this."

"Yes, the photographer did an excellent job," her mother said, and her father was also happy with the layout.

"The ad will start running next Wednesday. It will also appear on the Internet. Interested buyers will have the opportunity to complete the invitation form and submit it to our platform. We will forward all forms to your e-mail address," the editor said.

"Wonderful," Christine and her parents said simultaneously. They each shook hands with the editor and thanked her for a first-rate job.

"I feel so bad for being late."

"No harm was done, Christine. The meeting you had must have been very important," her father said.

"A client is thinking about starting a home-based business and needed information on how to start a corporation but discovered, through no fault of his own, that he did not own the house, which is about to go into foreclosure. He became frantic. I had to ease his mind and advised him to contact a lawyer to straighten out the mess."

"There seems to be a lot of that going around, people losing their homes because they took on more than they could afford," her mother said in a conceited manner.

"Mom and dad, it was great seeing you. I will talk to you tomorrow about getting the house ready for viewing." She kissed her parents, got into her car and drove home.

Christine lived in a condominium, which her parents owned, in Park Slope. It was a one bedroom/one bath duplex with floor to ceiling windows, patterned flooring and an enclosed terrace. The unit was completely soundproof and close to shopping and major subways and buses. In two months, she would turn twenty-five and in due course would purchase the unit from her parents.

She could not believe how frisky she was with Awesome. Raised to be reserved when it came to sex, she became a wild thing last night.

He brought out all those hidden desires in me. It first happened when I walked into the classroom. No man has ever had that kind of sway over me. If I did not know it then, I know it now. Awesome is going to my husband. No matter how my parents feel about him, he will be mine.

Chapter 15

Awesome had all of his documents ready, went to the courthouse and filed the quitclaim deed. As Christine instructed him to do, he requested a certified copy of the certificate.

Next, he contacted Webster. "I am leaving the courthouse. I have to make a couple of stops but should be home after 3 p.m. Let us get together this evening."

"I'll be there around five."

When he got home, Awesome was on cloud nine. Now the proud owner of the house, he called *Home Financial Services* to see how much his parents owed. "Thirty thousand dollars," the representative said.

There was no way he could come up with that amount of money. His parents closed the business, checking, and savings accounts. Now in a state of panic, he called Webster and told him what had occurred.

"Are you home?" Webster asked.

"Yes."

"I am on my way." Webster arrived at the house in forty-five minutes. "Your parents owe how much?"

"I was shocked too when the man quoted that figure. I have ninety days to come up with the money. My checking account does not have enough money to pay for one month, much less six months."

"Call Christine and explain the circumstances. Let her take it from there."

"Webster, I will make that call tomorrow."

Chapter 16

It was Friday, and Christine was getting the place ready for the open house, which would take place tomorrow from 1 p.m. to 5 p.m. So far, one hundred people responded to the ad from the newspaper and two hundred from the Internet.

Her mother would greet the guests and hand them colorful brochures. To prevent bogus names and identification numbers, everyone would have to sign in and show a driver's license or a New York State photo ID, which would be handled by two security specialists. Christine and her father would chaperone potential buyers. The house was now ready for all to see.

Thinking about Awesome, Christine wanted to spend the evening with him. She called him. "Hi, I miss you and want to see you."

"You must have read my mind. I was going to call you. Would you like to come over now?" he asked.

"Yes, I will be there in one hour. I have a stop to make. Can I bring anything?"

"Just bring you."

She stopped at her parents' house to inform them that the house was all set for tomorrow. "Good, your father and I will be there at 9 a.m. The DJ will select the music to play throughout the house. Nothing stimulates a buying mood than high-quality melodies."

"Fine, I will be there at 10 a.m." She kissed her parents and left, heading straight to Awesome's house.

When Christine arrived at the house and rang the doorbell, she was stunned when Awesome opened the door. He was naked as a jade bird and his manhood stood at attention, as though he were a knight ready to engage in an erotic encounter. "Come in, milady." Laughing, she almost fell to the floor.

"Awesome, you are crazy." She raced into the foyer, removed her clothing and ran ahead of him, dashing up the stairs and into the bedroom. Like a dog in heat, he was in pursuit of her; the two landed on the bed. He got on top of her, pushing his stiff manhood inside of her. The gush was building up. She became an untamed sexual prowess, screaming, "More, more! I want more!" It was as though she was possessed by some erotic force.

"Baby, please, slow down," he pleaded, but his appeals were ignored.

She caressed and gripped his entire body. Again, he thrust himself inside of her; he thought that would slow her down, but it just added more fuel to the fire.

You want to play rough? Well, here I come.

He probed, prodded and aroused her to the point where she screamed, mercifully, "Hump, hump, hump me all night." The lovemaking lasted for six hours.

When Christine woke up, it was seven in the morning. She was bright-eyed, bushy-tailed, and ready for round two. "Awesome, wake up; let's do it again."

Are you kidding?

He came up with a quick response. "Honey, my back is hurting. I must have pulled a muscle. Can we pick up where we left off later?"

"You're no fun. Besides, I must leave and get ready for an open house this afternoon," she said, pouting.

"Speaking of house, I must talk to you about the loan my parents are obligated to pay?"

"Sorry, I will be busy for the next several days. When I can fit you into my schedule, I will call you and choose a date for our meeting." She kissed him on the forehead and left.

I see what you are trying to do, he thought. *You want to punish me for not giving into your demands. Well, two can play that game.*

He called Webster. "Listen, I can't believe that woman. She had me going for six hours."

"What! Is she on some kind of sex enhancement drug or is she just a super freak?"

"I don't know, but if I am going to be in her good graces, I will need a prescription for that blue pill."

"If you really want it, I can get it for you. I know this physician who will provide samples for a price."

"I'll let you know."

"When are you going to see her again?"

"She claims she'll be busy for the next several days. I believe she is trying to get back at me because I would not have sex with her this morning."

"This would be a good time to get plenty of rest and eat lots of high-energy bars, so you will be ready for her, you lucky dog." They both chuckled.

"Yeah, you are probably right. Webster, I will talk to you later."

Chapter 17

The open house was a success. Thanks to Christine's impeccable presentation, ten people showed an interest in buying the house. Her elegant words, beauty, and sophistication captivated likely buyers. Without realizing it, she had a way of charming and holding individuals' attention when she spoke. Her parents saw this early on, the effects she had on people. For these reasons, she became the spokesperson for all of their open house events.

When the Baileys sold a property, they never used a real estate broker. This is how they made their money, not having to pay silly commissions to ravenous agents. Brokers would have drunk contaminated water to get the couple's homes listed with their agencies.

A week later, the Baileys met separately with each of the ten possible purchasers. Three were offering 2 million; four individuals proposed 2.25 million; two were bidding 2.50 million, but the tenth person was willing to pay three million dollars in cash. None of the others could match that price.

The house was sold for three million dollars, and the money was wired into the couple's joint account. The proud owner of the house was an investment banker who traveled between New York and Bangkok.

For her excellent work, Christine would receive a three hundred thousand dollar bonus. "Because of you, the house was sold at a premium price," her parents said in agreement.

"Thank you, mom and dad. I will put this money to good use."

Christine was craving for Awesome but was penalizing him for refusing to make love to her. *Using this approach will make him want me more*, she thought.

Growing up, she would hear how some wives in her community would hold back sex when they were angry with their husbands. "Honey, I have a headache" was a popular excuse. Christine never wanted to play this type of game, because this sort of ploy could backfire, giving justification for husbands to have extramarital affairs. As she got older, she recognized that most men never needed a reason to cheat; they just did it on a whim.

Maybe his back was bothering him, she thought. *After all, I was vigorous with him. I think I should call Awesome before I end up losing him for good.*

It was 8:30 a.m. when Christine called Awesome. Groggy, he answered the phone. "Hello."

"Good morning, sweet pea. Did I wake you?"

He recognized her voice but decided to get back at her by playing a spiteful joke. "Nice hearing from you, Carmen. I had a great time last night. I would love to see you again?"

"I am sorry. I must have dialed the wrong number."

"Gotcha, Christine. How do you like me now?"

"Awesome, I deserved that. I was annoyed with you that morning and apologize for being such a brat. How is your back?"

"You are beautiful when you're angry. It is a turn-on. My back is much better."

"Good, I am glad to hear that. Which day is good for you to discuss business?"

"Today would be perfect."

"I can be there in twenty minutes."

This time, he was fully dressed and thought, *I do not want a repeat performance and will wait until I know where I stand, money wise, before going to bed with that nymphomaniac.*

Awesome saw her coming into the yard. He took several deep breaths before going downstairs. Instead of ringing the bell, she tapped on the window. He opened the door and was awestruck by her. She was wearing a gray suit and sensible black pumps.

"It is nice to see you." She extended her hand to shake his. He was somewhat amused by her business-like mannerism.

Why is she being so formal? Awesome wondered and said, "As always, I am glad to see you. Let us go into my office and get down to business." He had all his papers organized on the desk.

She looked at the quitclaim deed and said, "Good job. Did you call *Home Financial Services*?"

"Yes, I did. So far, my parents owe thirty thousand dollars. Unfortunately, they closed all of their bank accounts. The money they took probably would not have put a dent into that obligation."

"I will pay the remaining balance owed on the mortgage and will invest in your business as a silent partner. Finding space will not be difficult. You can choose one of my parents' commercial properties. Are you in agreement with this arrangement?"

Do hens hatch eggs? "Yes, I accept your proposal, and thank you for believing in me."

"I will have my lawyer draw up the partnership agreement. You can have your attorney read it before you sign it."

She extended her hand to shake his. "I look forward to a long and healthy joint venture. I must go now and will send a check made out to *Home Financial Services.* Give my regards to your parents and tell them not to worry about anything."

Like hell, I will, Awesome thought. "You have a wonderful day too." He watched her drive off and called Webster but got his voice mail. "We are on our way to the land of milk and honey."

Chapter 18

The next day, Webster returned Awesome's call and asked, "What's up?"

"She is going to pay off the mortgage and provide me with the capital to start the business."

"Are there any strings attached?"

"Probably, but I will be two steps ahead of her."

"So, what's next on the agenda?"

"You can have Boris look over the agreement and make certain it benefits me more than her. He will not have to meet with her in person."

"When will the contract be ready?"

"She will call me."

The doorbell rang. "There is someone at the door. I will talk to you tomorrow."

It was the mail carrier with two special deliveries. One was from the Internal Revenue Service and the other from New York City Property Tax Division. When he read both letters, he roared like an angry lion. His parents owed fifty thousand dollars in back taxes to the IRS and ten thousand dollars to the city.

After calming down, he realized Christine would take care of this. After all, she agreed to pay off all debts pertaining to the house, but to be sure, he called Webster to get his opinion. "It's me again. The house is in arrears for back taxes."

"If it weren't for bad luck, you wouldn't have any luck at all," Webster said, lightheartedly.

"I will have to mention this tax thing to Christine."

"How much tax is owed?"

"Sixty thousand dollars."

"Wow! Let her pick up the tab. After all, she seems to have it bad for you and will do anything to keep you in her life. So work your magic on her."

"Stop it Webster," he said, laughing. "I will talk to you sometime next week."

"Peace, brother."

A week later, Awesome received a registered/certified letter from *Home Financial Services*:

November 20, 2007

Dear Awesome Petté:

We are writing to thank you for paying the remaining balance of the mortgage. The house is clear and debt-free.

Please make certain that you keep this letter in a safe place in case questions arise about the ownership of the property.

Attached are all the documents pertaining to your case. It gives us great pleasure that you did not lose your home.

If we can ever be of assistance to you, please do not hesitate to contact us.

Very truly yours,

Benjamin Anderson
Loan Modification Specialist
Home Financial Services

Awesome called Christine, thanked her but said, "I received a letter from the IRS and the city giving notice that taxes are owed on the house."

"How much is owed?"

"Sixty thousand dollars: fifty thousand dollars to the IRS and ten thousand to the city."

"I will take care of it. Can I come over this evening?"

"Sure you can."

"I will bring my checkbook," she said ecstatically.

"And I will order something special," he said, purring like a sly cat.

Awesome ordered grilled chicken, collard greens, and cornbread from *Joe's Chicken Joint*. He had a bottle of champagne on ice and was ready for whatever Christine was going to throw at him.

Of all the women he bedded, she was the first who knew how to please him to a point of no return. Taking the lead was always his job, but because he needed her money, he was willing to let her be the principal player in the bedroom. In fact, he would let her roll all over him until he got what he wanted.

He looked out the window, saw her crossing the street and went downstairs to let her in. "Hi, Christine, you look stunning in that yellow dress."

"Why thank you, sir. I do declare; you are a vision for sore eyes." They hugged and kissed each other. She felt his hard pecker against her. Before he realized it, she placed her attaché case on the floor, took off her dress and removed his clothes. They got as far as the living room and settled on the plush carpet with her on top of him.

"I am so happy everything worked out for you. I explained to the loan officer that your parents transferred the house to you. And because of my name and the influence my parents have, I was able to have the paperwork completed faster."

"Christine, you are a pearl." He picked her up, carried her up the stairs and into the bedroom. On the bed, he spread her legs apart and inserted his stem inside of her. "This is my gift to you. I thank you from the bottom of my heart." An insidious smirk ran across his face when he made that statement.

After two hours of steamy lovemaking, they both reached the best climax of their lives. "Christine, you have stirred my appetite. It is time to eat."

After finishing dinner, Awesome showed Christine the letters from the tax agencies. She got out her checkbook and wrote out a check to each entity. "I will always be beholden to you," he said, smiling.

Chapter 19

In four weeks, Christine would turn twenty-five and have access to her trust fund, which was twenty-five million dollars. She could only withdraw a certain amount of money each year until she reached twenty-eight. If she got married before then, all of the money would be at her disposal.

Her lawyer drew up the contract for Awesome's start-up business. She would invest two million dollars and help locate a place for his operation. Finding a spot would not be difficult since her parents owned several ideal properties.

She made the call. "Good morning, Awesome, the agreement is ready. If it is okay, I will bring it over now."

"*Bonjour*, my divine queen. I cannot wait to see you," he said with an ominous glee.

"I will be there in a hop, skip, and a jump."

Before he could move, the doorbell rang. It was Christine. "Did you fly here?" he asked in shock.

"No, I was across the street in my car and was going to surprise you but thought it would be better to call first."

Thought it would be better to call first. What is this woman up to? Awesome wondered. "Well, I am always delighted to see you."

She took out the agreement and gave it to him. He read it over. "Everything looks fine, but I will have my lawyer examine it."

"If your attorney has any questions, he can contact my lawyer. Here is his business card. I cannot stay. I have an important meeting. It was nice seeing you."

"Likewise, and I will contact my lawyer right away." They kissed. She left, got into her red Porsche with tinted windows and drove off.

I have never seen that car before. It must be brand new.

He called Webster. "Hey, I have the silent partnership agreement. Can I come over there? Can you get Boris to meet with us?"

"You are in luck; he is here."

"Great, I am leaving now."

Awesome was now suspicious of Christine. He could not get over the fact that she was in front of his house when she called him. *I have to be extra careful with that sneaky one.*

No one knew this, but his house had a secret back entrance with a long pathway, which headed into different directions. On one side were private homes and a twenty-one-floor complex; on the other side were restaurants, shops, and a park.

If Miss Bailey thinks she can park in front of my house, watch me when I leave and follow me, boy, will I have a shocker for her, he thought. *She will be sitting in her car for a very long time.*

Webster and Boris were watching TV when Awesome arrived. "Hi, Boris, it is good to see you."

"Good to see you too. I understand you have a contract for me to read."

"Here it is. Tell me what you think."

"I must say, your lady friend has covered everything. What is good about this contract is that she will not be active or have any say in the running of the business. The only problem I see is that she will not be personally liable for any debts or other obligations. I recommend that you ask her to assume these responsibilities until you see a profit. Let's say five years."

What Boris did not know was that Awesome did not intend to be with Christine that long. He had other big plans.

"Thank you, Boris. I will have her make that change."

The next day, Awesome called Christine. "My lawyer looked over the contract and suggested you be liable for all debts and obligations for at least five years to give me leeway to make a profit." He kept his fingers crossed, hoping she would accept that suggestion.

"I will agree to that on one condition."

"And what is that," he asked, holding his breath.

"That you let me move in with you."

Taking in a mouthful of air and exhaling slowly, he said, "You beat me to the punch. I was going to ask for your hand in marriage?"

Pausing for a second, she replied, "I will have my lawyer add that clause and bring the contract for you to sign tomorrow. Goodbye, and have a nice day."

My goodness, she wants to move in with me, but I might have blown it by mentioning the M word, Awesome thought.

The following evening, Christine came over with the revised contract. She and Awesome signed it. From her tote bag, she removed a bottle of Chardonnay and two crystal wine glasses inscribed with his and her name. She opened the bottle, poured the wine and made a toast: "I wish you nothing but success."

"Thank you." He took her upstairs to the bedroom and started to make love to her.

"Yes," she said. He thought she meant yes, keep it up.

"Yes, I will," she kept repeating.

"Yes, you will what," he asked again.

"Marry you." After they reached their best erotic moment, they fell asleep.

Awesome woke up the next day, but Christine was gone. On his nightstand was a cashier's check for two million dollars. He looked out the window to check for a red Porsche, which was not there. He did not want to take any chances, so he left through the secret door, went to the bank, opened a business account and deposited the two million dollars.

Yippy aye, everything is falling into place.

Chapter 20

Christine called Awesome. "I have found a place that I know you will love. Would you like to see it now?"

"Sure."

"I'll be there in twenty minutes to drive you there. I don't want you getting stuck on the road in that old wreck of a car."

Prior to meeting Christine, he could not afford to buy a new or used car. Webster would tease him about that jalopy, which Awesome bought for three hundred dollars. Sometimes the car would stall; it cost more to tow than the vehicle was worth. Thanks to Christine, he now has the money to purchase a brand new car for personal and business use.

Located in downtown Brooklyn, the store Christine had in mind was perfect; it was close to subways and bus lines, office buildings, shops and restaurants. *Second Hand Treasures* would attract affluent shoppers and individuals seeking old and contemporary things.

When Awesome saw and walked into the two-story structure, it exceeded his expectations. The building had a front and back entrance, an enclosed garage and an elevator. On the top floor was a one-bedroom unit with 12 feet ceilings, bare brick walls, hardwood floors, a state-of-the-art kitchen with a dishwasher, a custom master bath with separate shower, and a laundry room, which came with a combination washer and dryer.

On the main floor was a 1,500 square feet showroom. Then you had the 2,500 square feet basement for storing supplies, office equipment and merchandise. The shop was the perfect front.

"Do you like it?" she asked.

"What's not to like."

"Then, this is all yours."

"What do you mean this is all mine? Don't your parents own this building?"

"Not any longer, here is the title deed and the keys. If you wish, you can rent out the top floor. As written in the agreement, I will take care of the taxes, utilities, insurance and any other expenses until your business begins to make a profit."

"I do not know what to say or how to thank you, Christine. You have been too generous," he said.

"You have already asked me to marry you. That is thanks enough."

She drove him back home. "I will give you enough time to digest all of this and will call you next week." They kissed. She left and drove off in her car.

Awesome called Webster. "This plan is working far better than I anticipated. It is time for us to have our first official meeting."

"When and where would you like to meet?"

"Let's meet at my shop next Friday."

"What shop?" Webster asked.

"You'll see." He gave Webster the address. "How does 10 a.m. sound?"

"That's fine. I will see you then."

Awesome drove up to his shop in a blue Lexus. Just so happens, Webster was already there. "When did you buy that car? It is smoking."

"Two days ago. I paid cash and drove it off the lot."

"You paid cash?"

"That is right. Christine gave me the money for the business, so I treated myself to a nice used car. If I am going to sell second-hand stuff, I must practice what I sell."

"Not any used car, but a second-hand Lexus," Webster said, shaking his head.

"As they say, 'go big or go home.' How long have you been standing here?"

"I got here about ten minutes ago."

"Let us go inside. You know, she bought this building for me."

"No way did she buy this building for you." Awesome handed him the deed.

Webster looked at the document but could not believe his eyes. "Gee-whiz, she is really into you."

"I am not done. She accepted my marriage proposal."

"She did not!"

"Yes, she did."

"Well, shut my mouth. Have you set a date?"

"I am not going to rush things until everything is in place."

"Don't take too long; she may become impatient," Webster said.

"Let me give you the tour." They went upstairs where the apartment was. "I could rent this floor for at least two thousand a month."

"Or maybe more," Webster said. They went to the main floor, which was ideal for displaying the merchandise.

"Let's check out the basement, where you will be working."

"I cannot believe this entire scheme is falling into place without a hitch," Webster said.

"And the best is yet to come," Awesome replied, winking.

Awesome had Webster design a sign for the shop. *Second Hand Treasures* was now on the map. Filled with knick-knacks, the shop's grand opening would take place in one week, just in time for the holidays.

Most of the items came from Awesome's house. His parents had ancestral masks, carvings, and sculptures that were brought over from the island. When they renovated the house, they added modern and old furnishings and other ornaments from various estate sales.

Webster's high-quality laser printers, scanners, video cameras, cell phones, and other essential materials were in the basement. Advertising in newspapers or distributing flyers to passersby would draw too much attention to his work. Even though his operation was away from prying eyes, Awesome would have to know whether customers were there to shop or to have phony papers made.

While going over last minutes specifics, the two came up with a solution. Anyone seeking Webster's service would say the following, "Mr. Sharp referred me to this place."

When Webster started his business, he was working out of his two-bedroom apartment. Most of the tenants knew the nature of his business; some of the neighbors were his best customers, referring relatives and friends who needed his service.

Yet, he still had to watch his back. People talk; envy can rear its ugly head. Someone can break into your home and steal your equipment or money. Worse, law enforcement is breaking down your door, hauling you off to prison, and the individuals who benefited from your work have disappeared.

For these reasons, Webster jumped on board when Awesome came up with a plan to use a legitimate business as a cover. Without her realizing it, Christine Bailey was the perfect pawn for this ruse.

While the two were getting ready to leave the shop, Awesome's cell phone rang. It was Christine. "Hi, boo."

"Hello, honey. It's so nice hearing your sultry voice."

Webster was whispering, "Stop your shucking and jiving." Awesome smiled.

"I was just leaving the shop. I hired a company to make a sign for the store. Most of the merchandise is here. I just have a few more particulars to iron out; everything will be ready for the grand opening."

"Good, don't forget to save all of your receipts."

"Would you like to come to my house this evening?"

"Yes, I would," she answered.

"Why don't you come over after six," he suggested. "I have a few stops to make."

"That works for me."

"Okay, Christine, I will see you then."

"Webster, before we leave, I need you to print out some fake invoices for your truck, which delivered the items and for the sign."

"Consider it done." Webster printed two bogus proofs of purchase: one for *Sharp's Trucking Company* and the other for *Signs Unlimited.* "Here they are."

"These are perfect. I will give these invoices to Christine this evening."

Chapter 21

Christine was sitting in her car when Awesome arrived home. As he was getting ready to unlock the door, he had an eerie feeling. When he turned around, she was standing behind him. "Good evening, my love."

"You should never sneak up on a person like that. I could have mistaken you for a mugger."

"And what would you do? Tackle me to the ground and make love to me."

My goodness! This woman is weird. "No. I would scream for help," he said, laughing robustly.

She started to laugh too. "Awesome, you are funny. That's what I love about you; you have a wicked sense of humor." They went into the house. She was wearing a pair of black leather pants.

This outfit will definitely turn him on. If it doesn't, then I will have to change my modus operandi.

"As always, you look divine." *Like a dominatrix*, he thought. "Did you bring your whip?"

"There you go again with your naughty sense of wit."

"I have those receipts for you." He was not in a sexual mood and wanted her to take the statements and leave.

"You don't have to give me invoices every time you purchase something. Wait until you have an accumulation of bills."

"That makes sense."

"I see you bought a new automobile."

"Actually, it is a used car."

"You are amusing and frugal."

"I don't want to end up like my parents, getting into debt for living beyond my means." He saw himself as a snake oil salesman when he made that statement.

"Awesome, you must not think that way. You have a good head on your shoulders; you will not end up like your parents," she said, sauntering up the stairs.

Where is she going? I hope she does not think we are going to do the nasty. He went into his office, acting as though he was attending to business.

Then, he heard her voice. "Awesome, I am waiting for you." Reluctantly, he went upstairs and into the bedroom. Stretched out on the bed, she was butt naked with a can of whipped cream in her hand. He had no choice but to yield to her lustful desires.

The whipped cream accomplished its function. He understood what Christine really wanted. It did not matter if it was him or someone else; she wanted a man in her life, a man who could enable her to release all of those pent up sexual wishes. As long as he fulfilled those needs, he would have free rein over her mind, body and soul and her funds.

Awesome woke up first. When he reached over to look at Christine, she had a smile on her face. He could not tell if she were awake or still asleep. "My little pussycat, are you awake?" She did not respond. "Sleepyhead, it is time to get up."

"Good morning," she said, placing her tongue into his mouth. "How did you sleep last night," she asked.

"Like a baby. I must get up and tend to business. With the grand opening around the corner, I must meet with an associate and go over last minute marketing and promotional ideas for the shop."

She got out of bed, took a shower and dressed. Before leaving, she went into his office. "After the opening, we must discuss my moving in and our wedding plans."

"That is a good idea," he said, acting as if he were excited about her suggestions.

"Oh, by the way, my parents will be attending the event. I have not told them about you being my lover but a client. I'll have to break it to them gently." She kissed him on the forehead and left.

Sounds like her parents are going to be a problem.

Christine never talked much about her parents. He gathered they were somewhat firm when it came to her upbringing. She once said, "My parents were very strict when it came to the boys. If they could, they would have made me wear a chastity belt." Based on that comment, he understood why she was a fanatic in bed. Her floodgates were bursting at the seams.

All he knew about the Baileys was what he read in the newspapers or heard from the town criers, who saw them as ruthless and money hungry. One individual referred to the couple as "fiends in the flesh."

As far as Awesome knew, his parents never met the Baileys, and if they had, they never mentioned it to him. After meeting their daughter and from some of the remarks she made, he understood his mom and dad would have never been part of that clique.

His parents did not come from old money but came to this country with enough determination to chase that American dream, which became a nightmare.

He guessed the Baileys would probably never give him a second look nor welcome him into their loop.

The mere fact that Christine has to introduce me as a client rather than as her boyfriend says quite a bit. I already have her under my spell. If push comes to shove, I will probably have to call in reinforcements to neutralize her parents.

It was after 11 p.m. when Awesome went to bed. The next morning, he called Webster. "Listen, Christine is planning to bring her parents to the grand opening. We will have to put together a plan that will keep them out of our business. If you have nothing planned for this afternoon, let's get together."

"Do you want me to come to your house?"

"No, let us meet at our usual watering hole. How does 2 p.m. sound?"

"I will see you then," Webster said.

Chapter 22

Webster was good at evaluating people. He could tell if an individual was really well off or faking it, honest or corrupt or easily bought off and understood how to use these components to take advantage of people.

As a kid, he traveled with his father, who was a door-to-door salesperson, selling costly vacuum cleaners to homemakers.

When it came to looking for people's weaknesses, his father was an expert. The minute he stepped into a woman's home, he knew she was desperately looking for attention. These women were some of his best customers because he did more than just sell them a product; he gave them what they really wanted: electrifying sex.

His father's sale pitches were enticing. He won top salesperson of the year for five straight years. An affair developed with one of his female regulars. Eventually, the two ran off together, leaving Webster and his mother to fend for themselves.

A year later, Webster's mother remarried and moved to Nevada, leaving her son behind. He had just graduated from high school and started working at the printing company. On the side, he began homing in on his con artistry skills. Therefore, if anyone could figure out the Baileys, it would be Webster Jones.

Awesome and Webster sat at the bar mapping out their scheme for the grand opening. Webster would pretend to be a successful businessperson, observe the Baileys and initiate a conversation with the couple. Awesome would hire some people and provide them with money to purchase a few items from his shop.

"Everything seems to be in place," Awesome concluded.

"I can't wait to play my role," Webster said, singing his own praises.

They both had a drink in their hand and made a toast. "May we both be drowning in wealth," Awesome whispered.

"I'll drink to that," Webster responded.

Today is the grand opening of *Second Hand Treasures*. Store hours would be from 9 a.m. until 6 p.m., Monday through Friday and Saturday from 11 a.m. until 7 p.m. Awesome arrived at the shop early and wanted to make sure everything was in place, making certain no mishaps would occur.

Fifteen minutes later, Christine called. "Good morning, Awesome, I will not be there when the shop opens. Due to a last minute emergency meeting, my parents and I will be there this afternoon between one and two. Remember, I will be introducing you as my client and not as my fiancé."

He was baffled because their engagement was not official since he never gave her a ring, but he would go along with the parody. "I did not forget what you said the last time we were together."

"My parents can be difficult if they don't know anything about you or your family," she sighed.

And they never will. "Since I am not from high society, are you saying they will not like or accept me?" he asked, pretending to be hurt.

"Awesome, please don't take offense. They are old-school snobs and can be too protective when it comes to the men in my life. I am not like them. You know that. I do not care how much money you have or do not have or who your family is. I love you for who you are."

"Sweet thing, I am not upset, and I love you for being your true self. I will see you when you get here."

He called Webster. "Hi, Christine just called. She and her parents will be here this afternoon between one and two."

"No problem, I know what they look like. I came across their photos while researching them online. I will be sitting in my car. When they enter the shop, I will follow."

There must have been twenty people waiting for the shop to open. Most of the people were from Awesome's roll. The remaining bunch would come at various times throughout the day and weeks until the shop was attracting real customers.

Shoppers were impressed with what they saw. A few wanted to place some of their unwanted items on consignment.

Christine and her parents finally arrived. Awesome greeted them with a phony smile. "Welcome to *Second Hand Treasures*, Christine."

Shaking his hand, she said, "This shop is lovely. You have a winner here."

"Thank you, from your lips to God's ears," he replied.

"Mr. Petté, I would like you to meet my parents, Mary and James Bailey."

"It is a pleasure to meet you." He extended his hand but neither one of them shook his hand.

Her parents were not impressed with him or his shop. "All I see is junk," Mary said to James.

Awesome did not hear Mrs. Bailey's remarks, but Christine did. "Please, mother, do not be impertinent. Mr. Petté is my client. He put his heart and soul into starting this business."

"Christine, your mother did not mean any harm," her father said, expressing regret for his wife's commentary.

Awesome approached Christine and her parents. "Please, have a look around. If you are looking for something unique that you do not see, let me know. I will try and get it for you. As you will see, over ninety percent of the merchandise is sold."

"What made you go into this line of business?" Mr. Bailey asked, acting as if he cared.

"I heard someone say, 'you can make a lot of money selling cast-offs.' I did my research and decided this would be a great money-making venture."

"Well, all I can say is good luck."

"Thank you, Mr. Bailey." *You SOB.*

Chapter 23

Webster was waiting in his car. After allowing enough time for the Baileys and their daughter to browse *Second Hand Treasures*, he took a last minute glance at himself in the mirror. Looking like an aristocrat, he got out of his car, crossed the street and walked into the shop. With an English accent, he said, "I would like to speak to the owner of this establishment."

His brogue and gesture blew the Baileys away. To say they were in admiration of him was no lie. "Christine, do you know that gentleman?" her mother asked.

"No, I have never met that man. Why do you ask?"

"He maybe someone you need to meet," her father highlighted.

"Why?"

"My dear, I can see he is a man of class and means."

The Baileys went over to Webster. "Hello, sir, we could not help noticing your accent. Are you from England?"

"No, my parents are. I was born here and picked up the drawl from them. They are now living in Barbados. Are you the owners of this fine shop?"

"No, that man in the blue suit is the owner. He is my daughter's client. I am Mary Bailey, and this is my husband, James."

"It is nice to meet you. My name is Manny Smith."

"Christine, come over here and meet Mr. Smith," her mother insisted.

"Excuse me, Awesome." She went over to her parents.

"Christine, this is Mr. Manny Smith."

"Nice to meet you, Miss Bailey," he said, extending his hand.

"It is a pleasure to meet you, Mr. Smith." She shook his hand and said, "Pardon me." Leaving her parents and Mr. Smith, she went back to continue her conversation with Awesome.

"Mr. Smith, what is your line of business?" Mary asked.

"Please, call me Manny. My parents own an auction house, which sells artwork to wealthy collectors. I travel the world looking for unusual pieces for their enterprise. I will only be here for a couple of days, heard about this place and thought I would check it out. As a matter of fact, I see something over there."

"That is very interesting, Manny. My husband and I are in the real estate business. Perhaps we can get together for dinner before you leave and discuss how we can help each other."

"I would like that. Do you have any plans for this evening?"

"No."

"There is a nice restaurant across the street. Would you like to meet there, let's say, around six?"

"Perfect, we will see you then."

"Well, let me go over to the owner and bid on that painting."

The Baileys went to their daughter. "Christine, your father and I are leaving. We are having dinner with Mr. Smith at six this evening at the restaurant across the street. Why don't you join us?"

"Thank you for asking, but I will have to decline. I have a previous engagement, but you enjoy your dinner with Mr. Smith."

"Okay, if you change your mind, you know where we will be."

Webster had the Baileys where he wanted them. He did not have to say much. By listening, he learned a lot about the couple. It was obvious to him the two led separate and personal lives but were united when it came to business.

James was born in Georgia, had that old southern charm and spoke eloquently but would stab you in the back if it meant putting more money in his and his wife's pockets.

On the other hand, born and raised in Mount Vernon, Mary was urban chic and a true socialite, but behind that veneer was a woman who could probably chew nails and spit rust and not give it a second thought.

The waiter came to the table and took their order. "It will be a thirty-minute wait for your food, which our chef prepares from scratch. Would you like to order a drink now or wait?"

"I can wait," Webster said.

"We will order an after dinner drink."

"As you mentioned, you and your husband are into real estate. What type of properties do you own?"

"We buy commercial structures and old homes and renovate them into spectacular buildings and estates, which sell from six to seven figures."

"I have been thinking about buying a brownstone and using it as a rental property. Here's my business card."

"If you would like to see some of our homes for sale, we can send you videos by e-mail. I see you have two e-mail addresses."

"Yes, the top one is for personal mail and the other is for business."

"Would you need financing," James asked.

"No, I would pay cash. I already have two homes in Barbados."

When he made that statement, the couple's eyes intensified. "Would you reside in the home or be an absentee owner?" Mary asked.

"Since I travel over ninety-five percent of the time, I would be an absentee proprietor."

"Well, if you decide to buy one of our homes or a house from another realtor, we can act as your property manager."

"That sounds excellent. It would take the pressure off me trying to find renters, collecting rental fees and tending to complaints. I would pay you to take care of any unforeseen problems."

"We manage all of the buildings we own, don't just rent to anyone and do a thorough background and credit check. We only rent or lease to the crème de la crème," James emphasized.

"No riff rats living in your properties," Webster said. When he made that comment, the couple shook their heads in agreement.

"We have never had any problems with our residential or commercial tenants. The majority of our renters come through people whom we have worked with or have known for years."

"I will have no problems providing you with business and personal references or my credit history."

"We have no doubt about that. Just looking at and listening to you, you are a man of integrity."

"Why, thank you." Webster had to hold back the glee.

The waiter came with the food, which was excellent. The restaurant had a five-star rating; critics would give rave reviews about the food and service. This was the first time the Baileys had eaten there. "James, we must come here again. Mr. Smith, thank you for recommending this bistro."

"It was my pleasure."

"Would you like to order your drinks?" the maître d'
asked.

"My husband and I will have the coffee liqueur."

"I'll have gin and tonic." The waiter came back with the
drinks. Putting on airs, Webster asked for the check.

Objecting, James said, "Mr. Smith, this is our treat."

"That is very kind of you. The next time, I will pick up
the tab."

Mr. Bailey took out his credit card and handed it to the
server. The bill was two hundred and fifty dollars. It was
9:15 p.m. when Webster and the Baileys left the restaurant.

"I see *Second Hand Treasures* is closed. Before I leave, I
will have to go back to see if the owner is willing to come
down on his asking price for that painting," Webster said.

"Whatever he is asking is probably too much," Mary said
in a stuck-up tone. "It was so nice meeting you, Mr. Smith.
My husband and I are looking forward to doing business
with you. You have a safe trip home."

"Thank you, until we meet again," Webster said, waving
goodbye.

Chapter 24

After closing the shop, Awesome and Christine drove straight to his estate. They were relaxing on the love seat in the spacious living room. "What did you think of my parents?" Christine asked, stroking Awesome's face.

"They come over as very lovely people. The question is what did they think of me?"

"I did not have a chance to talk to them, but once they get to know you, they will end up loving you." Realistically, she knew her parents would never accept him based on the remarks her mother made about his shop. He did not come from a prominent family, so they would do everything in their power to discourage her from being with him. Moreover, marrying him would be the ultimate dishonor.

"Awesome, your shop did well on its first day of opening."

"Let's hope the momentum continues."

"If today was any indication, your shop will make a profit sooner than you projected."

"You are probably right. Sales totaled twelve hundred dollars," he said, beaming. "Let's celebrate. I have a bottle of champagne in the refrigerator."

"I will go upstairs. Don't take too long, *Mr. Don Juan.*"

Awesome took his time walking up those stairs. When he went into the bedroom, Christine was sitting on the edge of the bed with her legs spread opened; she was wearing a mask and a string of pearls around her neck.

Great googa mooga! This woman is full of surprises. Even though he was exhausted, he was ready for her, because he had a job to do, keeping her happy with non-stop succulent sex.

When Awesome woke up, it was seven in the morning. Christine was snoring.

Good, he thought. *She is still asleep. Let me run into the shower before she wakes up.*

He was not fast enough; he heard her stirring and turned to face her. "Good morning, morning glory. Where are you rushing off to?" She was wet as can be. "Come over here and give me some sugar," she petitioned.

"Baby, I must get to the shop early. I am expecting a delivery."

"Please, Awesome, please. It won't take long to satisfy me." He took gratification in the way she begged him for sex.

"Okay! Brace yourself. I'm coming." He placed his hardness inside of her and took her on a wild erotic expedition.

For thirty minutes, they moaned, bumped and massaged each other, reaching a sizzling and dripping climax. The two kissed, got up and showered. Christine dressed and decided to go home. She embraced Awesome. "I will see you in a couple of days. Have fun at the shop. If you need anything, call me."

"Thank you, I will. Have a great day."

Awesome could not wait to get out of that house. No one enjoyed sex more than he did, but Christine was over the top horny. He had to come up with a way to slow her roll but not to the point where he would end up losing her and the money.

When he arrived at the shop, Webster, masquerading as Mr. Smith, was waiting. "Good morning, Mr. Smith. Are you still interested in buying that painting? The price you wish to pay is too little."

"I know, Awesome, but fifty dollars is too high for a silly looking picture, no matter how old it is."

"Webster, is that you?"

"Yes, it is little old me."

"Let's get inside before someone recognizes you."

"Who is going to recognize me? You didn't," Webster said in jest.

"Damn! I'll be a monkey's uncle. I had no idea that was you with that fake accent, makeup, mustache, and spectacles. I truly thought you were a genuine customer who wanted to buy that hideous watercolor."

"And I never had any acting lessons. Who would have guessed it?"

"Who did your makeup, and how did you come up with the accent?"

"Boris, he is a jack-of-all-trades and a master of most. Besides taking some acting classes, he also learned to do makeup and talk in various enunciations. So I got him to transform me into an English gentleman."

"I saw you talking to the Baileys but did not give it a second thought. You never told me how you were going to tap into the couple's psyche."

"Ah! I had those conceited idiots eating out of my hand. They even introduced me to your significant other. Perhaps, they thought I would be a great match for their daughter."

"It was clear her parents did not like me, especially her mother," Awesome said. "She never acknowledged me, but her husband did inquire how I got into this business."

"Her husband does come over as someone who would show an interest in the junk business, but I would not trust him as far as I can throw a hippopotamus."

"I wonder how Christine ended up with parents like them," Awesome asked.

"You two are going to be husband and wife. Mark my word."

"Now that I have money for the business, I can buy Christine a ring to make the engagement official."

"Don't worry about purchasing a ring. I know a jeweler who makes house calls. He owes me a big favor. When you are ready, I'll call him, and he will bring an assortment of rings for you to select."

"Let us keep this pretense going until you leave the shop. You never know who is watching. One morning, Christine was outside my house; she was sitting in her car. She probably thought she would catch a woman coming out of my place."

"You are right, but I will not have to carry on this charade after today. I told the Baileys I was leaving the country tomorrow. When I do business with them, it will be online."

While Awesome and Webster were talking, a couple walked into the shop. "Good morning. As soon as I finish with this customer, I will assist you. Please look around."

"Mr. Smith, let me get that portrait and pack it for you." Awesome went behind the counter, wrapped the item and rang up the total. "That will be fifty dollars." Webster smiled and handed him five ten dollar bills. "Thank you for patronizing *Second Hand Treasures*. It was a pleasure serving you. Please tell your associates about this shop."

"I will. *Cheerio*."

The couple purchased two tribal masks, four silver bangles, and two handcraft wooden statues and spent over one hundred dollars.

When Webster left the shop, he decided not to drive home. He knew the manager of a motel, which was a ten-block walk. He went there and checked into a room. If anyone followed him, there would be no suspicion on the person's part since he was a traveling businessman.

He removed his makeup, accessories, and clothes and placed them into a plastic bag. He changed into his regular wear, left the room and tossed the bag into the compactor.

Chapter 25

December 21 was fast approaching. It would be Christine's birthday. Awesome felt the perfect gift would be an engagement ring. He called Webster. "I would like to see your contact about a ring."

"When and where?"

"I think the shop would be perfect. Tuesday would be ideal. Her birthday is next Friday."

"I will call him and set up the appointment."

Second Hand Treasures' earnings for the week were five thousand dollars. Whatever money Webster made, whether legal or illegal, Awesome would receive fifty percent. That money would go into a secret account at another bank, which Christine knew nothing about.

He decided not to rent out the apartment but to use it to store merchandise since Webster's equipment and supplies were taking up most of the space in the basement.

If Christine asks, he would explain that he is using the barter system, allowing a printing company to use the basement in exchange for designing and printing materials for marketing and promoting *Second Hand Treasures*.

There would be no need for her to go into the underground room, and if she did, she would not suspect anything.

On Tuesday, Awesome met with the jeweler, who had a collection of high-quality rings.

"You may pick any of these gems, compliments of my company," the jeweler said, smiling.

Awesome was confused. "I don't understand."

"I am beholden to Mr. Webster Jones, so this is my way of paying him back. Do you see what you like?"

"Yes, I like this yellow stone."

"Good choice. This is one of our popular gems. It is somewhat flawed but still beautiful, especially if you are on a tight budget. The weight is one carat. What size would you like it in?"

"I forgot to measure her finger. I want it to be a surprise; her birthday is next Friday."

"That will not be a problem. I believe this size should do. Most of our female clients choose this dimension. I will provide you with a ring guard in case the ring it too big. If it is too small, we can resize it at no cost to you. Here is my business card."

"Sir, I thank you for your assistance."

"It was my pleasure. Congratulations to you and your fortunate lady." The jeweler left and disappeared into the crowded street.

An hour later, Webster came into the shop. "How did it go with the jeweler?"

"Here's the ring I picked. Do you think she will like it?"

"That is stunning. If she doesn't like it, something is wrong with her."

"Webster, I was taken aback when he said there was no charge. I expected to pay something."

"Don't worry. That man is making millions because of me. The least he could have done was not charge you."

"How much do you think this ring is worth?"

"Looking at it, it is probably worth anywhere from two to three thousand dollars. To be on the safe side, have it appraised. If it turns out to be a zirconia, he will have to answer to me."

The next day, he took the ring to have it assessed. Webster was right; the diamond was valued at twenty-five hundred dollars. Awesome received a certificate of authenticity for the rock.

Awesome wanted to make plans for Christine's birthday. Rather than take her to a restaurant, he would have a special dinner at his home and hire a catering service to put together an intimate dinner for two.

He wanted to make certain she did not have any plans for that day, so he called her on Wednesday. "Hi, sweetheart, I am just checking to see if you have any plans for your birthday."

"Hello, baby, my parents are taking me out to dinner. They made reservations at a fancy restaurant in Manhattan. I would invite you, but I do not want them to become suspicious of our relationship. Can we get together this Sunday?"

"Sunday is fine. Be at my home at 6 p.m. I will plan something special for you."

"I'll be there."

"Enjoy your birthday with your parents."

"Thank you. I will try my best to have a good time. With you not there, it will be hard putting up a good front."

"We will have plenty of time to make up for lost time. *Adieu*, my little tart."

"*Au revoir*, my love," she said.

Imagine that, she knows how to say goodbye in French.

After getting off the phone, he called the caterers and explained his wishes. They were very obliging. Everything was set for Sunday. He then called a cleaning service to come in on Saturday to get the living room and dining area in tip-top shape.

It was now Friday. Before heading to the shop, he called Christine to wish her a happy birthday. Delighted to hear his voice, she could not wait to see him on Sunday.

Awesome drove to Queens to purchase some woodcarvings, a silver teapot and stand, a Tiffany lamp, an antique clock, and a crystal punch bowl with matching goblets from a couple who was putting their house up for sale. Their asking price was one hundred dollars for the items. Getting rid of the objects was more important to them than making a windfall. He carefully placed the objects into the trunk of his car.

While driving back to Brooklyn, he thought about Christine and her stuck-up parents. *When will she put her big girl panties on and stand up to them? It is not as though she relies on her mom and dad for financial support. If she were able to give me two million dollars and the commercial building, why care what they think?*

It was 8:15 a.m. when he arrived at the shop. He parked near the side entrance of the building, removed the items from the trunk of his car, took the elevator to the upper level, removed and tagged each article and brought them downstairs to display.

Friday turned out to be a good day. At closing time, there was hardly anything left in the shop. Revenue for that day was one thousand dollars.

Webster was downstairs getting ready to leave. Since the cleaning crew was coming to Awesome's house tomorrow, he would not be coming into the shop and asked Webster to put a closed sign in the shop's window. Besides, there was not that much in the store for anyone to buy, just a few tables and chairs.

"Awesome, don't worry. I will take care of everything. You and Christine have a great birthday."

"Thanks, Webster, and you enjoy your weekend."

On Sunday, the caterers arrived at 4:30 p.m. They did a beautiful job decorating the table and went that extra mile by placing party favors and streamers throughout the dining area. In the foyer was a banner that read *Happy Birthday, Christine*.

The menu included filet mignon, home-fried potatoes, steamed asparagus, and toasted baguette. Dessert would be lemon sponge cake topped with rum sauce. He wanted the night to be just right.

A happy woman will be more generous with her money.

He did not want the two waiters to serve dinner. He would take care of that himself. The heating plate would keep the food warm.

Before leaving, one of the servers placed a bottle of champagne in an icer, compliments of the catering service. Awesome thanked the staff for doing such a superb job and gave each person a one hundred dollar tip.

The doorbell rang at 6 p.m. sharp. It was Christine Bailey, looking sexy as always and wearing a long fur coat and knee-high leather boots.

Why is she wearing a fur coat? It is not even cold outside. We have had mild temperatures since the beginning of December.

"Good evening, Awesome."

"Good evening and happy birthday, my little sugarplum."

Christine saw the banner on the wall. "That poster is adorable." She then followed him into the dining room. "The table is beautiful and that cake looks divine."

"I had everything catered and wanted this day to be just right for my little kitten." After he made that remark, she removed her coat and dropped it to the floor.

Great balls of fire, this woman is unbelievable. She was butt naked, except for those boots she was wearing and those tassels hanging from her nipples.

"Shall we sit down and eat," she asked in a seductive voice.

"Yes, have a seat." He started to serve the food.

She took a bite into the steak. "This is juicy; biting into this meat is like making love," she said, moaning and groaning.

Is she insinuating that she wants to have sex right this minute? What type of mix messages is she trying to send me? Awesome wondered. "I am glad you like it, but the best is yet to come."

"And what might that be?" she asked, licking her fingers and lips.

"You will see after we have dessert."

"Can we get to the dessert now?"

"But you haven't finished your meal."

"Let's go upstairs and have our cake and eat it too." She got up from the table and ran up the stairs. He just sat there, shaking his head. He placed the leftover food into the refrigerator and understood dessert for her meant engaging in tropical forest lovemaking.

The sex lasted until midnight. Awesome was surprised; he was not tired and neither was Christine. If they wanted to, they could have gone another round.

This would be a good time for me to present my next surprise to her. He went into the drawer and pulled out a red velvet box.

"Christine, this is my gift to you."

When she opened the box, she started to scream. "Is this what I think it is?"

"Yes. Again, will you marry me?"

"For the second time, yes," she said, weeping for joy.

"It is official. We are now engaged," Awesome said, pretending to be in high spirits. He opened the champagne and poured the bubbling wine into two glasses and made a toast to his blushing fiancée.

"Awesome, you have made me the happiest woman on earth. I am counting the days when we become never-ending soul mates."

Keep that momentum going, my silly one.

Chapter 26

Christine was full of bliss. In addition to getting that beautiful rock, she was now able to tap into her trust fund. There was one problem. How was she going to break the news to her parents?

No way in hell will they accept Awesome into the family. There is only one solution. We will tie the knot at City Hall and disclose the news to my parents afterward.

It was Christmas Eve. Awesome was planning to close the shop early. It was a slow day, which brought in five hundred dollars. Webster had a last minute job to do for an important client and would be there until midnight.

"Got any plans for Christmas Day," Webster asked.

"No. Christine will be spending Christmas with her family. So I will be spending the day alone."

"What is it with your fiancée; she did not invite you to join in the festivity; when is she going to tell her parents about you?"

"From what I can see, she is afraid to alienate them. They will never accept me and will do everything in their power to keep us apart or from getting married. That's how much influence they have over her."

"If that is the case, what do you think your life will be like after you marry her?"

"I don't plan to stay with her that long. In any case, you enjoy your holiday, and don't work too hard."

"You enjoy your day," Webster replied, returning to the basement to begin working on his project.

When Awesome arrived home, he called Christine to wish her a Merry Christmas. Instead, he got her voice mail. As he was about to go upstairs, the doorbell rang. It was his fiancée, giggling as though she had hit the lottery. "I came to wish you a Merry Christmas."

"I thought you would be spending Christmas Eve with your family."

"I am, but thought I would come by first and give you your gift."

"You did not have to buy me a present. You have already given me so much."

"Come outside." There was a minivan parked in his driveway.

"What! You didn't!"

"Yes, I did." She handed him the bill of sale and keys and signed the title over to him. "Now, you don't have to use your Lexus to transport merchandise to and from your shop. I cannot stay, but you have a great Christmas. I will see you after the New Year."

After the New Year! Did I hear what I thought I heard?

"My parents decided to fly to Atlanta for the holidays and asked me to come. I could not say no to them. We are leaving on a private jet this evening."

"I did not know your parents own an airplane."

"They don't. The plane belongs to a colleague, who happens to be going to Atlanta. At the last minute, he asked us to join him. My father has family there. I have not seen them since I graduated from college, so it will be a big family reunion. I am so sorry you won't be there."

As if I really care. Who wants to be around uppity folks?

"I see. Well, you and your parents enjoy your trip and have a great family get-together."

"Thank you for understanding." She kissed him, got into her car and drove off.

Awesome stood there in amazement, gazing at his new vehicle. The black van came with side doors, a rear door, front door, front seat, and an enclosed back area for hauling small to medium sized items. For larger or heavier objects, he would use Webster's truck.

Chapter 27

Awesome was busy tallying the week's receipts, which was one thousand dollars. Webster was doing phenomenal business. His revenue for the week was five thousand dollars with half of that going to Awesome. *Crime does pay*, he thought.

It was New Year's Eve. He had not heard from Christine since Christmas Eve, the day she bought him that big-ticket item. He was thinking about her, was going to call her but changed his mind.

A female customer came into the shop. "Good evening, Mr. Sharp referred me to this place."

"Go straight to the back, and take the elevator to the lower level."

"Thank you," she said, smiling.

It was near closing time. Just as Awesome was about to close the shop, a couple walked in. They wanted to buy a depression era punch bowl set displayed in the window. The asking price was one hundred dollars. They were willing to pay fifty dollars. He accepted their offer.

Whatever he wanted for an item, he would double or triple the price, knowing most buyers will haggle for a lower price. Many of the customers who came into the shop were looking for pieces to add to their collections. Others were seeking rare antiques to sell to auction houses.

Awesome could not believe how some people would pay an exorbitant amount of money for an object that seemed worthless. Yet, he never forgot what a collector once said, "It is worth what some damn fool is willing to pay."

The young woman who came to see Webster left. He came up fifteen minutes later. "Man, I am done for the night; stick a fork in me. Have any plans tonight?"

"No, I am going home and straight to bed."

"Alone?"

"Yes, alone."

"I will see you next year," Webster said.

"Don't do anything I wouldn't do."

Webster exploded into laughter and said, "You have a Happy New Year, Awesome."

"You do the same, Webster."

When Awesome arrived home, it was almost ten o'clock. He got undressed and showered. When he came out of the bathroom, he heard the doorbell chime. *Who could that be this time of night?* After putting on his robe, he went downstairs. When he opened the door, he was in a state of shock.

It was Christine. "Surprise…! I would never let you bring in the New Year alone," she said, hugging and kissing him. "My goodness, you are drenched. Did you miss me that much that you had to take a cold shower?"

"You are too amusing. I thought you and your parents weren't due back until after the New Year."

"I decided to come back. I could not stand being away from you any longer."

"I am glad you are here. I still have some champagne left over from your birthday. Let's go upstairs and bring in 2008 with a bang."

It was a night of orgasms gone haywire. Christine and Awesome went at it for several hours without taking any time out. She saw the New Year as the turning point of her life and was no longer going to allow her parents to dictate whom she should or should not marry. She took out her calendar and said, "I want you to pick a date for us to get married."

"How does February 14 sound?" he asked.

"Done," she said.

"Where would you like to have the wedding ceremony, and how many people do you want to invite?" he asked.

"We are getting married at City Hall and without guests."

"Don't you want your parents to be there?"

"No. After we are married, we can have a nice reception and invite our parents, relatives, and friends. We will fly your parents in."

He liked the idea of going to City Hall. The last thing he wanted was a big wedding or being around characters that he did not know. As far as having his parents at the reception, he would have to get Webster's friends to play his mom and dad.

Awesome went online to see what information he would need to fill out the application for the marriage license. The only thing he did not know was where his parents were actually born. He had not heard from them since they left on July 27, 2007, and doubted if he ever would.

Webster knew people who had connections to Martinique and asked one of them to make up false birth records for Awesome's parents. That bit of information would mysteriously show up in their hall of records. His father's date of birth would be January 3, 1956; his mother's date of birth would be September 26, 1958.

One week before Valentine's Day, Awesome and Christine went to the Office of the City Clerk to get an application for a marriage license. They presented proper identification and completed the form. The office processed their marriage license while the couple waited. When the processing was completed, they received their marriage license but had to wait twenty-four hours before they could get married.

Awesome had house keys made for Christine. She was now starting to move some of her personal effects into the house; she would hold off buying the condominium from her parents but would keep the unit completely furnished, as though she were still living there. In the interim, her parents would be in the dark about where she was really residing.

She adored every part of her fiancé's home. Even though he sold a lot of his parents' furnishings, the house was still a work of art. For now, she would not have to beautify the place.

Everything Christine ever dreamed about was coming to fruition. In a couple of days, she would be Mrs. Awesome Petté, the wife of a successful capitalist.

My parents will admire him once they get to see who he really is.

It was Valentine's Day. The couple woke up at the same time. Christine was jubilant. Awesome wanted to make love to her. "Let's wait until we are married. It will be more special," she said.

More special. Is this woman for real? All of a sudden she wants to wait until we are legally hitched. Going along with her silly request, he said, "You are right. This is an extraordinary day."

"Awesome, there is something I have to discuss with you."

"Can we talk later? It is already 7:30. I want us to get to City Hall before the doors open, so we can be the first ones there."

"Okay, but remind me when we get back home. It has to do with my trust fund."

Trust fund! What trust fund? She never mentioned any trust fund. Wait a minute! Does she want me to sign a prenuptial agreement? No. She would have brought that up before now.

The temperature was mild. Christine had chosen a white silk dress to wear. Awesome had a black suit with a red tie. They would drive to the shop, park the car in the garage and walk to the municipal building. None of his or her friends would attend the ceremony. Webster's two partners in crime would play the role of witnesses. The marriage had to remain a covert affair.

It took about an hour before the officiant performed the civil ceremony, which was simple and to the point. "...I now pronounce you husband and wife."

At the conclusion of the service, Awesome took the witnesses to the side, thanked them and handed the man an envelope, containing two hundred dollars. The man and his female accomplice left the building and disappeared. Christine assumed the couple was employed by City Hall to be observers for couples who did not have their own personal witnesses.

After receiving the Certificate of Marriage Registration, Christine and Awesome went back to the shop to get his car and drove home.

Awesome carried his bride over the threshold, took her to bed, and made love to her. When they woke up, it was 8 p.m.

"Honey, I must talk to you about my trust fund."

"What trust fund," he asked with a stunned look on his face. *Did my parents ever think about setting up a trust fund for me?*

"The trust stipulated that at age twenty-five, I would have access to twenty-five million dollars but could only draw out a certain amount each year until I reached twenty-eight or got married, whichever came first; now that I am married, I can take out as much money as I want. If you need additional funds or want to expand into other ventures, the capital is there."

Awesome could not believe what he was hearing. He still could not understand why she did not have him sign a prenuptial agreement. "My dear, that is nice to know." *You have just made my day. How do I count the ways to use twenty-five million dollars?* "When do you plan to tell your parents about us?"

"I plan to invite them to dinner."

"Where are we going to take them for dinner?"

"Here," she said.

"Don't you think it would be better to have them at your condominium where it is more intimate?"

"I do not understand. Our home is beautiful. Besides, they will be in awe with you and this estate, knowing it was yours before we got married. I don't want them to think you married me for my money."

"What I am trying to say is that we have not had time to be in this house as husband and wife. I am not ready to share this place with your parents or anyone until we have been together for at least several months."

"Honey, I am so sorry for being selfish. You are right. Here I am planning an intimate dinner with my parents, and we have yet to plan our honeymoon."

"The honeymoon will have to wait. The shop has not been opened that long. If I close the shop for even one week, I can end up losing money."

"There I go again, thinking of my needs. The honeymoon can come later. Besides, being married to you is like being on a romantic voyage."

"We can pretend by doing special things every evening."

"That makes sense," she said, kissing him.

I always make sense, and with twenty-five million dollars at my disposal, I will be making plenty of cents.

Chapter 28

Christine took her husband's suggestion; she would have the dinner at her condominium and use the same catering service he used for her birthday.

She called her parents. "Hi, mom, if you and dad are not doing anything this Saturday, I would like you to come and have dinner with me. I have an announcement to make."

"Can you give me a clue," her mother asked."

"No, it is a surprise."

"All right, your father and I will be there. What time should we arrive?"

"Dinner will be served at 4 p.m."

When Awesome arrived home, the aroma from the kitchen enthralled his senses. "Hi, I hope you are hungry," Christine said, smiling. "I prepared your favorite chicken dish. Dinner will be ready in ten minutes." This was the first time she cooked a meal for him. Before they got married, it was always takeout.

"Yes, love, I am ravenous." When he went upstairs, he saw her sexy lingerie spread out on the bed.

I guess this will be my dessert. He changed into something more comfortable, came back downstairs, and went into the dining area, where dinner was waiting.

"I called my parents today. They will be at my condominium on Saturday at 4 p.m."

"Honey, the food looks scrumptious." He took a bite into the curried chicken and almost had a hard-on. It was simply mouth-watering. "My little muffin, you have outdone yourself. Where did you learn how to cook?"

"I will never tell. A woman must keep some secrets to herself. Do not expect this type of service every night. At least once a month, we must go out to dinner."

"It is a deal," he said with a devious beam.

It was Friday. Awesome told Webster he was closing the shop at noon tomorrow, which was one of the busiest days. He was going to face the firing squad. Christine was finally going to tell her parents about their marriage. "Man, I would like to be a fly on that wall," Webster said, laughing.

"But you haven't heard the best. My wife is worth twenty-five million dollars."

"Say what?" a bewildered Webster asked.

"She has a trust fund. Now that she is married, all of that money is hers and mine to do as we please. Better yet, she never had me sign a prenup."

"Are you kidding? You mean when you get a divorce, you would be entitled to half of the money."

"If I play my cards right, all of the money will be mine."

"Did she add your name to the trust account?"

"No."

"Awesome, how long are you going to stay with Christine?"

"Not too long, but a lot will depend on her parents. Once they find out we are married, they will do everything in their power to break us up or move her money to a safer place, where I can't touch it."

"What you need to do is to make certain she moves that money into a private account with your name on it. You should do this before she tells her parents about your marriage," Webster said.

"But we are seeing them tomorrow."

"Awesome, this is what you need to do: Call Christine and say your parents are planning to visit you in two weeks, and maybe it would be a good idea to postpone the announcement of your marriage until they arrive. This will give you enough time to get your wife to transfer that money into a joint account."

"That is an excellent idea. I will call her." He got out his cell phone and made that call. She was home. "Hi, baby doll, I have good news. I just heard from my parents. They are planning to visit me in two weeks. I did not tell them about our marriage but thought we should cancel tomorrow's dinner with your parents and reschedule it for another day so that both of our parents can be present."

"Awesome, that is great news. When will they be arriving?"

"I don't know. They will get back to me with that information."

"Wonderful! I will call and tell my parents that something came up and that I will have to put off our dinner meeting for another day. I cannot wait to meet your parents. Having them here will make the meeting with my parents more bearable," she sighed. "I will call the caterers and ask them to deliver the meal to our house. I won't have to cook for a couple of days."

"That makes sense. I will see you when I get home."

"Should I keep dinner warm for you?"

"No, I will grab a bite before I leave the shop."

"How did it go," Webster asked.

"It went as I expected. I have two weeks to get that money into a shared account."

Christine called her mother to inform her that she would have to cancel tomorrow's dinner. "There was a scheduling conflict. I forgot I had another important appointment at the same time, which I cannot change. It was on my computer. I had penciled in our dinner date on my desk calendar." She was good at coming up with quick explanations when she found herself in a bind.

"Fine, I will tell your father when he returns to the office."

"Give him my love."

"I will. Take care."

James had just walked into the office.

Mary: "I just got off the phone with Christine. Tomorrow's dinner is off. She accidentally scheduled two appointments at the same time. Lately, have you noticed how preoccupied our daughter has been? If I did not know any better, I would swear she is becoming forgetful in her young age."

James: "She is twenty-five and has access to heaps of money. This is a lot for her to handle at such a young age."

Mary: "Listen, Christine has a good head on her shoulders. We raised her to be very astute when it comes to money. She would never do anything to jeopardize her finances. The money she makes from her consulting jobs has grown to seven figures, so she doesn't need to touch that money in her trust fund."

James: "That may be true, but you realize there are goniffs out there that will try to take advantage of our baby girl because of her millions."

Mary: "We will never let that happen. She always surrounds herself with men who are financially on or above her level."

James: "Has she spoken to you about what she plans to do with the money?"

Mary: "No. She has an account at a brokerage firm; let them advise her. If she needs more guidance from us, she will ask. Remember, she can only withdraw a certain amount of money each year until she reaches twenty-eight; if she gets married, she can remove as much money as she wants."

James: "Do you know if she is seeing anyone?"

Mary: "I doubt it. If she were, we would know. Talk about a man in her life would spread quicker than spreading caviar on Melba toast."

After Christine got off the phone with her mother, she called the caterers and asked them to deliver the food to her estate instead of her condominium. "No problem," the woman on the other end said. "We'll deliver the meal at 4 p.m."

Awesome got home around eight in the evening. Christine was upstairs watching TV. "Is that you honey?" she yelled.

"Yes, my little dumpling. It's your lover boy." It was a busy day at the shop, and even though he was exhausted, he would use sex to direct her into discussing what she was planning to do with all of that money in her trust fund. On his way up the stairs, he removed all of his clothing.

Seeing his naked body, she said, "I am ready for Freddy. Come to momma and give me all you got." He got on top of her and drove straight into her. "Do me," she screamed, grabbing onto him like a leech.

"Maybe it is time for us to move that money from your trust fund into a joint account. If I need money for expanding the business, I will have access without bothering you," he whispered.

"Ah! That feels so good."

"So, we will go to your bank, first thing Monday morning, and move the money."

"Yes, we are husband and wife. What is mine is yours."

That is all he needed to hear. They both reached a climax at the same time and took a break. He went downstairs to get something to drink. Five minutes later, he came back into the bedroom. Again, the two went at it until they fell asleep. When they opened their eyes, it was Saturday morning.

Chapter 29

Since the dinner date with his wife's parents was not going to occur, Awesome decided to keep the shop open until closing time. Webster was already there making fake documents for a key client.

"How did things go yesterday?" Webster inquired.

"Christine called her parents and cancelled the dinner date. The story I told her about my parents coming here worked. We are going to the bank on Monday to transfer the money from her trust fund into a joint account."

"How were you able to get her to agree to do that so early in the marriage? I still can't believe she did not have you sign a prenup."

"Sex played a big role. You remember when we were in high school; we had girls eating out of our hands; whatever we asked them to do, they did it, and they never gave it up to us. They loved our aura, which was enough for them. Well, Christine is a different animal. She has to have it, and she would sell her soul to the devil to get incredible sex, the devil being me."

"Go on with your bad self," Webster said, snapping his fingers. "So what's next?"

"Once Christine transfers the money and adds my name to that account, I will make up some story that my parents decided to come later. While making love to her, I will give her some outlandish tale. As long as I keep fueling her honey pot, she will believe anything I say."

"So, her *Achilles' heel* is sex," Webster said.

"It is, and I intend to milk it until she can't stand it any longer."

"Fat chance that will ever happen," Webster concluded.

The shop was crowded with customers. Awesome decided to stay open an extra hour. So far, his take was nine hundred and fifty dollars.

A customer came into the shop with a painting, which she found in her deceased aunt's attic and wanted to put the piece on consignment.

"We do not do consignments." Awesome looked at the painting and asked, "How much do you want for this item?" An art of this nature was not one of his areas of expertise, but he recognized the piece had some value.

"Make me an offer," the woman replied.

"I can give you fifty dollars." She thought hard and long and accepted his offer.

He called Webster and asked him to come up for a second. "Do you have any idea how much this canvas might go for?"

"It looks like it might be worth a lot. I have a client who studies paintings. I'll call him." An hour later, the expert came into the shop.

Awesome showed the painting to the man, who gave it a once over and said, "You can easily get two hundred dollars. I know someone who would be willing to buy it." With his cell phone, he took a picture of the image and sent it to a potential buyer. Ten minutes later, he handed Awesome the money, took the painting and said, "It was nice doing business with you."

Gee-whiz! I should have more days like this, Awesome thought. He gave half of the two hundred dollars to Webster. They always made a pact that if either one of them made money from a referral, they would split the money fifty/fifty.

Chapter 30

When Awesome woke up Monday morning, Christine was in the shower. He went to join her. The warm water pulsating against their bodies was exhilarating. He felt he had her right where he wanted her. "Honeybee, I was thinking."

"Stop thinking and make love to me," she insisted.

"Listen, I am serious. Perhaps we should open a new account at another bank. Your parents know the administrator at the bank that manages your trust fund. What we are doing may get back to your parents before we have a chance to talk to them."

"Do you have a bank in mind?" she asked.

"Yes, my parents' bank."

"Okay, if it makes you feel any better, we will open an account there with both our names and have the money moved there. You should also know that I have a brokerage account at my bank, which has five million dollars, and your name will be added to that account too."

The commercial bank was four blocks from their home. Since his parents once had a business and checking account there, the manager was glad to assist the newlyweds. Awesome and Christine opened a joint account. "I will wire thirty million dollars into this account in a day or two," she told the manager.

The two went back home. Awesome thought it would be a good idea for Christine to go to her bank without him. "No one will be suspicious if you are alone." She went to her bank and arranged to have all of the money moved to his bank.

Awesome went to his shop. When he checked his voice mail, there was a message from Christine. "Hi, everything has been taken care of. The money is on its way to our new joint account. I am on my way home and will see you this evening."

It was after eight in the evening when Awesome got home. When he went upstairs, Christine was fast asleep. He was glad because the last thing he wanted to do was make love to her.

He went downstairs and into the kitchen. There was still some food left from Saturday. He placed the vegetables and chicken in the microwave and started to think about his future without Christine.

Half of the investment he received from his wife for *Second Hand Treasures* was sitting in an offshore account. He would have to be very careful when it comes to taking money from their joint account.

Christine slept through the night. When Awesome woke up, she was still asleep. He quietly got out of bed, showered and dressed. When he checked on her, she was snoring. It was already 7:30 a.m. He left the house and drove straight to the shop.

Webster arrived at the shop around 8:30 a.m. He had a big job to do for a man who needed fictitious ID cards for several of his relatives. "How did everything go at the bank?"

"I convinced Christine to open a joint account at my parents' bank. She instructed her bank to wire all of the money into our account. It usually takes about three days to complete the transaction."

By the end of the week, *Second Hand Treasures* pulled in more money than anyone had imagined. Since its opening in November, sales topped over twenty thousand dollars. Half of that money came from Webster's business, which Awesome never entered into the books but wired into his secret account.

Awesome called his bank to check to see if the thirty million dollars was in their joint account. It was. Clapping his hands, he yelled, "Hallelujah!"

Webster heard him and came upstairs. "Awesome, what happened? You sound like you won the million dollar lottery."

"I did. The money from Christine's trust fund and brokerage account is now in our joint account. It is time for us to go to the next phase."

"Wait a minute! What brokerage account? Webster asked, scratching his head.

"My wife is full of surprises. She had five million dollars in that account."

"What other money does she have stashed away?" Webster asked.

"I don't believe there is more unless her parents have a secret account in her name, and if they do, we will find it."

Awesome arrived home late. He had a fake gloomy look on his face. "Christine, I have bad news."

"What is it, Awesome?"

"I heard from my parents. They will not be coming to New York. Something came up, which they would not go into. They felt very bad and apologized for getting my hopes up."

"I am sorry to hear that. I was looking forward to meeting your folks. Did you tell your parents about our marriage?"

"No, I did not think making that announcement over the phone was the correct approach. I rather do it face to face. It looks like it will be just us and your parents when you plan that surprise."

"As always, you are right. What if I call my parents now and see if they are free next Sunday?"

"That is a good idea. The sooner we tell them, the better. Our marriage will no longer be a hush-hush affair."

She made that call. "Hi, mom, how is everything?"

"I am doing just great. How are you doing? Are you taking care of yourself?"

"Yes, mom, I am. If you don't have any plans for next Sunday, I would like to invite you and dad to dinner at my place."

"I am sorry, but your father and I will be at Martha's Vineyard that weekend. One of our friends just purchased a home there. He and his wife are having an open house. However, we are free the Sunday after."

"All right, I will pencil you in for that day at 4 p.m."

"Are you certain you have no other activities for that day?" her mother asked in a curious pitch. "Remember, you had us and another engagement listed on the same day?"

"Yes, mom, I do remember, but this time, I checked my calendar and computer. You and dad enjoy your weekend at the open house. I will see you the following Sunday."

"Thank you, we will."

Christine went into the office where Awesome was going over some paperwork. "Sweetie pie, my parents are going to Martha's Vineyard next Sunday. I made the dinner date for the Sunday after at 4 p.m."

"Good, I am looking forward to that day." *Better yet, I cannot wait to see the look on their faces when you tell them we are husband and wife.*

Sunday turned out to be a beautiful day. Rather than use the catering service, Christine decided to plan and prepare the food herself. The menu included baked lobster tails, scalloped potatoes, tossed salad with basil vinaigrette, and strawberry gelato.

She wanted everything to be perfect. Having her parents at the mansion would have been her first choice, but she understood her husband's point of view. They were newlyweds; he wanted to share the home with her first. *It shows how much he loves and respects me.*

The table was stunning; the food looked divine. "Do you need any help?" Awesome asked.

"No, I have everything under control. Thank you for asking."

The condominium's doorman phoned. "Miss Bailey, your parents are here."

"Thank you, please, send them up."

"Is that your mom and dad?" Awesome asked, getting ready for the showdown.

"Yes." She opened the door to let her parents in. "Hi, it is so nice to see you. Let me take your coats. Make yourself at home." Awesome was in the bedroom waiting for his wife's cue to come into the living room.

"Would you like a drink? Dinner will be ready in thirty minutes."

"What do you have?" her mother asked.

"I have your favorite whiskey."

"I will have my drink with my dinner," her mother said.

"Me too," her father said, following his wife's cue.

"So what is this surprise you have for us?" her mother asked.

"Yeah, I have been on pins and needles," her father said.

"Well, I have fantastic news. I would like to announce that Awesome Petté and I got married on Valentine's Day." In a blasé manner, he slowly walked out of the bedroom and into the living room, as though he were a head of state about to address his royal subjects.

"It is nice to see you again, Mr. and Mrs. Bailey." Mrs. Bailey's mouth flew open like a flytrap, and Mr. Bailey was speechless as though the cat had gotten his tongue. "I fell in love with your daughter the first day she walked into the classroom. I promise to love, cherish, and protect her." Christine stood by her husband, holding his hand.

"Your face looks very familiar," her father said. "Have we met before?"

"Yes, we have. You came into my shop, *Second Hand Treasures,* with your daughter on our grand opening day."

"Oh, yes, I remember. We met that nice English gentleman there; you remember, Mary, don't you."

"Yes, I do. His name is Mr. Manny Smith."

"That's right, Mr. Smith, a notable man. How could I have forgotten his name? We had dinner that same evening at the restaurant across from your little shop. In fact, I have been thinking about him," Mr. Bailey said.

"Excuse me. I must go and check on dinner." Christine was furious with her parents at the way they were treating her husband. Minutes later, she came out of the kitchen and announced, "Dinner is ready."

"Your father and I were just reminiscing about Mr. Smith. We introduced you to him at your client's shop," her mother underscored.

"Mother, you mean my husband."

"My dear, he was not your husband then. I seem to recall you introduced him as your client."

"Yes, that is true, but I would like you to refer to him as my husband."

Awesome was proud of his wife, standing up to her mother. *At last, she showed some backbone. Stick that in your bonnet, Mr. and Mrs. Bailey.*

Throughout the evening, Christine's parents disregarded Awesome as though he were a stinkbug. Whenever they spoke, they never made eye contact with him. Mrs. Bailey took an instant dislike to him. Mr. Bailey was still in a state of shock.

Awesome decided to play the devil's advocate. "Mr. and Mrs. Bailey, Christine and I would like to invite you to our estate for dinner soon. In fact, we are thinking about having a reception and inviting family and friends to the celebration."

The Baileys never responded or looked his way. After finishing their meal, they were ready to leave. "It is time for us to hit the road. We have a big day ahead of us tomorrow. Dinner was lovely. Thank you for inviting us," her mother said. James just stood there like a lost little boy in the woods.

"You are welcome, Mr. and Mrs. Bailey," Awesome said, smirking.

"Mom and dad, thank you for coming. I hope you enjoyed yourselves." She walked them to the elevator and whispered, "I do hope you will give Awesome a chance and really get to know him. He is a wonderful man."

"It was quite an evening," her mother said. Her father said nothing. Christine went back to the apartment feeling disappointed.

"That was quite an evening."

"Awesome, I am so sorry. I never thought my parents would react that way."

"It did not surprise me. The way they treated me at the shop on the day of the grand opening, I did not expect them to welcome me with open arms, but I am not offended by their behavior."

"Well, I am. If they do not accept you as my husband, I will sever all ties with them."

What do you know? My girl is going to cut herself off from her parents. This is working out far better than I could have ever anticipated.

Chapter 31

Webster usually got to the shop around nine in the morning. He arrived early because he could not wait to hear how dinner went with Awesome and his wife's parents.

"Good morning. You're an early bird," Awesome said. "You have a big job to do?"

"No, I got here early because I am dying to know what happened yesterday with your in-laws."

"If you were a fly on the wall, you would have seen two people act as though I were dirt under their shoes. They never congratulated us on our marriage, never spoke directly to me but mentioned how much they admired you."

"Me, I have never met those people."

"You did, Mr. Manny Smith." They laughed until they could no longer express delight. "You made a good impression on *Mr. and Mrs. High and Mighty*."

"Imagine that! Maybe I should have been the one to marry Christine," Webster said.

"You may have given me an idea," Awesome replied.

"Please, leave me out of this drama. I have enough to deal with when it comes to the women in my life."

"Nah, I am playing with you. However, you can distract her parents by playing the role of Manny Smith again. You will not have to meet with them face-to-face. What I am planning for them can be done through other means."

"What's the plan for those two?"

"I will have to give it some more thought. It will definitely involve some of your contacts. Give me several more weeks to come up with a scheme. In the meantime, I want you to investigate the Baileys more thoroughly. People like them always have skeletons in their closets. If they don't, we will create them."

"From what I hear, they are ruthless and take no prisoners," Webster said. "You can be certain, if there is something explosive to be found, my connections will find it."

Chapter 32

The first undertaking Mary Bailey did on Monday morning was to call Danny Mayo. If it were the last act she ever did in her life, she would get that Awesome Petté out of her daughter's existence. She knew nothing about the man but it did not matter. He was not from or a part of their social class, so he had no right to be with their daughter. "What was she thinking?" she asked her husband.

"I want to know if she made him sign a prenup agreement," her husband expressed, rubbing his chin.

"Oh my goodness! If she married him on the *q.t.*, it probably never crossed her mind to discuss this with him."

Danny Mayo's voice mail came on. "Danny, this is Mary Bailey. It is very important that you get back to me as soon as possible. Millions of dollars are at stake."

If Danny learned anything from working with the Baileys, especially with Mary, there was never any excuse not to return a call the same day when one of them left a message. One hour later, he returned Mary's call. "How can I be of assistance to you, Mrs. Bailey?"

"We just found out our daughter got married."

"Congratulations, may your daughter and her husband have a long and happy life together."

"Congratulations, my petunias! I want you to do a detailed investigation on this man. His name is Awesome Petté; that is P-e-t-t-é," she said, seething.

"Can you give me additional information about this man? I will need to know where he was born, his date of birth and his social security number."

"I just told you; we know nothing about this individual. I doubt if our daughter knows much about this person." She had to think for a second. "Wait, he owns a junk store called *Second Hand Treasures* in downtown Brooklyn."

"This is something to go on. I will get right on it."

Is this man the son of the Pettés, whom I tried to find for their daughter back in September?

Danny did not care much for the Baileys, but he liked their daughter. She was nothing like them. She was kind and gentle, never judge people, did not care if they had money or not and would give away her last dollar to a person in need.

Should I tell her what her parents are planning? He thought long and hard and decided to call her. "Hi, Christine, this is Danny. I guess best wishes are in order."

She was puzzled and asked, "Best wishes for what?"

"Your parents told me about your marriage to Mr. Awesome Petté. They want me to investigate him. I am guessing he is not on their Christmas gift list. I wanted you to be aware of their request and check with you first before proceeding."

"Mr. Mayo, I am glad you called. I will double whatever they are paying you not to take this any further. They have no right to interfere in our lives."

"Understood; this is what I will do: I will make up a fake file on your husband but will never mention we had this conversation. You and your parents will be satisfied with the results."

"Thank you, Mr. Mayo. I will always be indebted to you."

Christine was angry. She called Awesome. "You must come home now!"

"Why?"

"It's my parents."

Did they fall off a cliff? "I'll be home as soon as possible."

He went downstairs to talk to Webster. "Listen, I must leave. Christine called asking me to come home. It has something to do with her parents."

"Were they beamed up by UFOs?" Webster asked, chuckling.

"I should be so lucky. Are you expecting anyone?"

"No."

"Can you take over for me while I am gone. I'll try to get back before closing time."

"If you are not here by then, I'll close the shop."

"Thanks."

Awesome rushed home. Christine was sitting in the living room weeping. "What's wrong, my little chickadee?"

"My parents hired someone to do a background check on you."

He had to think fast. "That's it. I have nothing to hide. My life is an open book."

"What if they discover your parents were behind in their mortgage, and they left you stuck with the bill, and you could not make those payments. My parents will conclude that you married me for my money."

"Let them assume whatever they want. If they believe I am a gigolo, then that is their problem not ours," he said, smiling. "Why would your parents tell you that they are doing a background check on me?"

"They didn't. The man they hired told me. He is the same man I hired to find your parents."

"What? Why would he tell you this? What he does for his client is confidential?"

"I guess he felt it was wrong to do this after the fact. He has known me since I was born. Nevertheless, I instructed him not to do anything. He will make up a phony report and submit it to me and then to my parents."

"Sweetheart, do not worry," he said, rubbing her back. "It will work itself out. If there is nothing else, I must return to the shop. I am expecting an important customer who wants to purchase some items that just came in."

"I feel so much better after talking to you. You always make a bad situation better." She kissed him.

"By the way, I did not get the name of the person your parents hired."

"Oh, his name is Danny Mayo."

Chapter 33

When Awesome got back to the shop, Webster was assisting a customer who wanted to purchase a cuckoo clock. "All right, I can take over."

"I'll be downstairs if you need me."

The price tag on the clock was one hundred dollars. The man only wanted to pay fifty dollars. Because Awesome wanted to get the shopper out of the shop, he accepted the man's offer. Since the buyer had his own truck, Awesome did not have to deliver the clock to his home.

After the man left, Awesome placed a closed sign in the window and went downstairs. "Webster, guess what?

Christine's parents hired a PI to investigate me, but she was able to stop him from probing into my life."

"How was she able to do that?" Webster asked with a quizzical gaze.

"The PI warned her before he started the job."

"What! He alerted her. Why would he do that?"

"Because he has known her since she was a baby, or maybe he felt what the Baileys were doing was wrong."

"Who is this PI?"

"His name is Danny Mayo."

"Danny Mayo! I have heard of him. He is one of the best in his field. Do you think you can trust him to do as Christine asked?"

"I don't know, but I do not want to take any chances."

"Don't worry. As we speak, my associates are checking into her parents."

"And while you are at it, ask them to delve into Danny Mayo's personal and business history. Let's find out what his weak points are."

It was after nine when Awesome got home. Christine was in the bedroom jotting down some notes in her appointment book. She had taken on a big consulting job, putting together a marketing and promotional package for a home decorating company that was planning to open in three months. "Hi, how did your day go?"

"It went great. More customers are coming into the shop through word of mouth."

"I am glad to hear that. I knew your business would be successful."

"Judging from the notes in your appointment book, you are going to be a busy little bee."

"Yes, I may have to travel to Atlanta in a few weeks. The company that I am helping is planning to open another branch there."

"That sounds interesting. With your knowledge and expertise, the company should do very well." *Moreover, you will be out of my hair.*

"Thank you, Awesome. I need that encouragement."

"Do you know when you will be leaving for Atlanta?"

"It will probably be sometime in April."

"How long will you be gone?"

"One week should do it. I wish you could come with me and meet some of my relatives on my father's side, but I realize you cannot close your shop now. You may end up losing customers and money."

"By the end of this year, I should be able to take some time off and visit your family. We can turn it into a honeymoon."

"Awesome, it's a deal."

I would not hold your breath if I were you, he thought.

She got undressed and rubbed her erogenous areas with Patchouli oil. He got naked. The two made love as if the end of the world was about to come.

Danny called Christine. "I have a made-up report, which I would like you to see before I send it off to your parents. I can send it to your e-mail address or have it delivered to you by courier."

"I rather have it sent to my condominium."

"Consider it done. It will be delivered after 1 p.m."

Awesome had already left for the shop. It was now 11:30 a.m. Christine got into her car and drove to her place. The package came at 2:30 p.m. She opened it and read the information. *Perfect, this should satisfy my parents.*

She called Danny. "Mr. Mayo, this is Christine. You did an excellent job on that report. Before you send it to my parents, I would like my husband to read it first."

"No problem, I will wait for your call."

When Awesome got home, she showed him the information.

"I am amazed. Mr. Mayo did a superb job; he made me look like a man of means."

"Honey, you are a man of means. You must remember my money is your money."

"No, your money is your money; my money is our money." *Oops, all the money is mine.*

"You are amusing," she said, caressing his body.

"Perhaps I should take my act on the road."

"I will call Mr. Mayo and tell him to send the report to my parents unless there is something else you would like him to add."

"No, your parents will be blown away when they read this." *With any luck, they'll be blown to kingdom come.*

The next day, Christine called Danny. "Go ahead and send the report to my parents. How much do I owe you?"

"Not a penny. This is on me."

"Thank you, Mr. Mayo."

"It was my pleasure."

Danny sent the information to the Baileys. He charged them five thousand dollars for doing nothing. He went online, saw a bio of a deceased billionaire and changed that man's name to Awesome Petté; he modified some of the details and downloaded the final vita, which he printed.

Awesome showed the report to Webster, who could not believe what he was reading. "This man knows how to con people. You think the Baileys will accept this?"

"If they are like most brash people, they will fall for it hook, line, and sinker."

The Baileys received the report on Awesome Petté. The more they read, the less they knew about this man. "Who would name their son Awesome?" Mrs. Bailey asked her husband. "If he is so rich, why haven't we heard about him before now?"

"According to this article, he is a very private person. It also says his family owns businesses and homes around the world but does not name the type of enterprises or their locations." As James continued reading the report, he reiterated, "We know he owns *Second Hand Treasures*. He may be a silent partner in some of those other ventures."

"James, you are probably right. I never thought of that. Many prosperous people are silent business partners. But I still don't understand why he and our daughter got married so quickly and didn't tell us."

"In all likelihood, Christine thought we would never accept him because he is not part of our circle."

"That may be true. But I am still cagey about this man and the marriage."

"Mary, for the sake of our daughter, let us get to know the man before we make any harsh judgments. She would be in a much better position to tell us more about him. After all, he was a student and a client of hers."

"I have the perfect solution," Mary said. "Let's give them a reception at *Ocean View Country Club*. What better way to get to know him by observing him in a social setting. With any luck, he will show us who he really is."

"That's a good idea. You are one smart cookie," James said, smiling.

Chapter 34

It has been two weeks since Christine's parents received the information on her husband. Not hearing from them, she could not tell if it was a good sign or a bad omen. She could not think about that now. She was planning to go on a business trip in several days.

Awesome was in his office going over revenues from the past week. The shop was doing well since its grand opening in November 2007. He estimated sales would continue to grow.

Christine was about to leave home when her cell phone rang. It was her mother. "Hi, pumpkin, you probably thought we had forgotten about you, but your father and I have been very busy. We just purchased two properties in Queens and will start renovating the homes shortly."

"Mom, it is nice hearing from you. I was just leaving."

"How is your husband?" her mother asked.

"Awesome is doing great."

"The reason why I am calling is that we would like to plan a reception for the two of you at *Ocean View Country Club*."

"That is nice of you and dad."

"Is Saturday, May 24, 4 p.m. to 8 p.m. okay?"

"I will have to check with Awesome and get back to you." She could not believe what her parents wanted to do.

"Awesome, you will never believe who just called."

"Don't keep in suspense. Who was it?"

"It was my mother. She and dad want to throw a reception for us at *Ocean View Country Club* in Westchester. They must have been in awe of Danny's report on you."

Either that or they are up to something. I would not trust them as far as I can throw a ship.

"It appears your parents are finally coming around to accepting me into the family. When are they planning this event?"

"How does May 24 sound? It would go from four in the afternoon until eight in the evening."

"I have no plans for that day."

"Good, I will make the call and confirm that day and time." She got the voice mail and left a message: "It's a go for May 24."

After Christine left the house, Awesome drove to the shop. Webster was already there. "Good morning, I have good news. Christine's parents are planning a party for us on May 24 at some highfalutin country club in Westchester."

"Get out of town," a stunned Webster said. "They are planning what?"

"You heard me. Her mother called this morning."

"What do you think they are up to, accepting you and your marriage to their daughter?"

"That is a good question. Christine seems to think Danny's report won them over. I beg to differ."

"Do you believe they are trying to set a trap for you?"

"No doubt about it. I will have to watch my p's and q's around her parents."

An excited Webster asked, "What can I do to help?"

"I have to think about that. Whatever we do, it will have to involve some of your contacts. Since her parents do not know where we live, we can meet at the house. You never know who is watching this shop."

"They still do not know where you and Christine live?"

"No, I assume they think we live in her condominium."

"You mean her condominium and yours."

"Not really. That condominium belongs to her parents. Therefore, I have no claim to it."

"I see," Webster said.

"Next week, Christine is flying to Atlanta on business. She will be gone for three days. During that time, we will choreograph our next move."

Chapter 35

A series of misfortunes were occurring, which were having detrimental effects on the USA economy.

During prior years, there was an increase in subprime mortgage loans with adjustable interest rates. As interest rates increased, so did monthly payments, resulting in mortgage delinquencies and foreclosures.

In many instances, people who had bad credit, no credit or insufficient income were receiving these types of financing. Millions of people lost their jobs. Household debt was higher than earnings. Wall Street tanked. Inevitably, these events led to a financial catastrophe and a serious recession.

On Christine and Awesome's block alone, several houses went into foreclosures, and there were more to follow. These owners were facing the same situations as Awesome's parents were in 2007, incessantly borrowing against their homes and owing more than what they could afford.

Housing prices fell, benefiting certain folks, namely the Baileys. They were buying up foreclosures faster than garbage trucks sweeping litter off the streets.

Second Hand Treasures was about to see a slump in sales. The people who would normally purchase big-ticket items were starting to dwindle.

Webster's business was going strong; many of his clients had disposable funds and were willing to pay big bucks to have counterfeit credentials made. Therefore, his business was sustaining Awesome's shop, not that the shop ever needed any financial support. His wife was paying all of the bills while he was lining his coffer.

While Christine was away on her business trip, Awesome and his team met at his home for an up-to-date status on Danny Mayo and the Baileys.

Boris Winston knew Danny quite well. The two grew up on the same block, although they each took different paths as adults.

Danny's father was a PI. People would refer to him as a decent and honorable man, who would often extend credit to people who were short on cash. When he died, Danny took over the business.

However, Danny's work ethics were a different story. He had none. "He could steal a gold tooth out of a dead man's mouth and sell the metal, claiming it was a good investment," Boris stressed. "He treated his staff like dirt and would cheat them out of their wages. It got to the point where he could no longer keep employees, so he ended up working alone."

"Most of Danny's work came from the Baileys," one of Webster's cohorts said. "He has worked with them for over twenty years, doing jobs that no one else would touch."

"The man forced some families, who were in financial hardship, to sign over their homes to the Baileys. Once those folks signed over their deeds, they became renters. Eventually, the Baileys would evict the occupants and sell those homes at obscene prices," another colleague alleged.

The biggest bombshell came when Awesome discovered that the Baileys owned the building that housed his parents'

Laundromat. "No wonder their daughter was so anxious to help me keep my house and invest in the shop," he said.

"Do you think Christine knew her parents owned that building?" Webster asked.

"She must have known. She is involved in the everyday running of her parents' real estate business," Awesome said.

"It does not mean she would have privy to all of her parents' holdings. They have their hands in so many pots; it is probably hard for them to keep up with all of their assets," Webster said.

The meeting went on until after midnight. The group decided to keep digging into the Baileys' background. "We have probably just scratched the surface. There has to be more to these two," Awesome pointed out.

"Are you going to mention to Christine about her parents' involvement with that building?" Webster asked.

"I will hold off on that until I receive more facts about her parents," Awesome replied.

Chapter 36

Mary Bailey was preparing for the big reception, which was going to be a day to remember. She called her daughter. "Christine, I will need a list of your husband's family and friends to invite."

"I will get that list to you soon."

"Please send that list by the end of this week. The day of the event will be here before you know it."

It was already April 7. Christine had just returned from her business trip. She was exhausted, working with the company's founder, who was about to open her doors in one month. With the economy in bad shape, she was not sure if the business in Atlanta along with its branch in New York

City would be able to maintain itself for the next five years. The promise of a loan to the company fell through. The last thing on her mind was some function.

She called Awesome at the shop. "Hi, my mother just called. She will need a list of the people you would like to have at the reception by the end of this week."

"There are only two people I would invite: my mom and dad. Hopefully, they will call me."

"I understand you have no knowledge of your other relatives, but what about your friends?" she asked.

"When I was about to lose the house and was low on cash, they all deserted me. You never know who your friends really are until you hit rock bottom. I have one friend who lives abroad. Sadly, he was in a skiing accident and will be out of commission for several months, so he will not be able to make it to the reception."

"I had no idea some of your friends abandoned you, and my heart goes out to your friend. I hope he gets well soon."

"It's okay. I have you, and that is all that matters."

"I will call my mother back and make up a story."

At the end of the week, Christine called her mother. "Mom, none of Awesome's relatives or friends will be able to come to the reception. It's too much of a short notice."

"I am sorry to hear that, but there will be other social celebrations." *That story is a bunch of bull. Christine, what have you gotten yourself into?*

Mary sent out five hundred invitations. Within two weeks, ninety-five percent of the invitees responded with a *yes*. She also took out a full-page ad publicizing the affair:

Mr. and Mrs. James Bailey would like to announce the marriage of their daughter, Christine Bailey, to Awesome Petté. The wedding ceremony took place on February 14, 2008. The reception will be held on May 24, 2008, at the Ocean View Country Club.

One week before the reception, Christine asked Awesome if he heard from his parents. "No, they have not contacted me. I think they are having financial problems. It seems as though the economic crisis has affected the whole world, including the Caribbean. I want to send them some money, but I do not know where they are. The phone number they gave me is no longer in service."

"I was looking forward to meeting your parents. It looks as though they will not be here to commemorate our union," Christine said with a gloomy expression.

"Buttercup, I must leave. You have a good day."

"You have a wonderful day too. Why don't we have dinner tonight at our favorite restaurant," she suggested.

"That is a good idea. I'll meet you there at 6 p.m."

While driving to the shop, Awesome noticed how some of the businesses had *retail space for lease* signs in the windows. The paper store around the corner from his shop closed its doors two weeks ago.

Awesome was displaying products in the window when a customer walked in. "Good morning, ma'am, how may I be of assistance to you?"

"Good morning, sir, I have some things that may be of interest to you. I will accept whatever you offer me," she said.

"Let's see what we have here," Awesome replied. There were four imported handmade dolls from the '30s, a locked chest with no key, and twenty comic books from the '40s, '50s, and '60s. He knew the comic books and the dolls were worth something but the chest was another story. "Do you have any idea what is in this box?"

"No, I found all of these items in the shed. A couple just purchased my home and wants everything gone."

"Do you have more items that you would like to sell?"

"As a matter of fact I do, but I am not sure if they would be a good fit for your shop. Most of the stuff is junk, which my deceased husband collected for the last fifty years. I plan to get a dumpster and trash everything."

"Well, junk is what we are all about. Where is the house?"

"It's in Stuyvesant Heights."

"Looking at these items, I can give you one hundred dollars, but I would also like to see what you have before you toss everything."

"I will accept your one hundred dollars," the woman said, smiling. Awesome handed her five twenty dollar bills.

"When would be a good time to come to the house?"

"I'll be home all day tomorrow." She wrote down her address and phone number on a piece of paper.

"Good, I will call you when I am on my way." He knew the homes in that community had some expensive heirlooms. What people see as junk, others see as a goldmine.

Thirty minutes later, Webster arrived at the shop. "Awesome, my man, what's happening."

"You just missed a customer. I gave her one hundred dollars for these dolls, comic books, and this chest, which I have no idea what it contains."

"Brother, you are slipping. There may just hot air in that box," Webster said, laughing. "But all kidding aside, the chest looks like it may be worth something. Look at its unique designs and patterns. They don't make stuff like this anymore."

"Webster, guess what?"

"What?

"The woman who sold me these items just sold her house, which is in Stuyvesant Heights; she has more effects that she wants to discard. I will be going to her place tomorrow to see what is worth salvaging."

"Will you need my truck?" Webster asked.

"I don't know. I will take my van. If there are items that are too big to load, I will return to her home with the truck."

Awesome placed the four dolls and the ten comic books in the window. He was about to take a break. Suddenly, a young man walked in. "Hi, I would like to buy all of those comic books." The price tag was one dollar each.

Around 5 p.m., another customer walked in. She bought the four dolls for one hundred dollars.

He went downstairs. "Hey, Webster, the comic books and dolls are gone."

"Gone, you mean someone shoplifted those items?"

"No, two customers bought them and they never tried to sway me to lower the price."

"You know what that means? You didn't charge enough."

"Probably not, but it does not matter. After all, this shop is only a front. It is not as though we need to make a bundle of money. We already have more than we expected."

"What are you going to do with that extra money?"

"I am treating my wife to dinner," Awesome said, snickering.

Chapter 37

Awesome and Christine arrived at the restaurant, simultaneously. They ordered a cocktail and selected the catch of the day: Grilled Salmon with Lemon Sauce.

"How did your day go?" she asked.

"Only two customers came into the shop. It seems as if everyone is affected by the recession." He did not want to talk about his business and moved her away from that discussion. "How did your day go? Will your client open her business as scheduled?"

"I am not sure if she will be able to open the second branch in Atlanta."

"One branch is better than none. Which city would benefit more from her company?" Awesome asked.

"I see both cities. You are probably right. Maybe she should concentrate on one office for now."

"Has the financial crisis hit Atlanta or New York the hardest?"

"It's difficult to tell. If you talk to some business people, they are doing fine, but others are about to call it quits. The problem is she may not get the loan promised to her from another source. Presently, we are not sure where things stand."

"Maybe she can hold off opening the company in Atlanta until the economy improves."

"That is a possibility, but who knows how long that will be."

"Let's enjoy our meal and not chat about business. Tomorrow is another day," Awesome said.

"I'll drink to that," Christine replied.

It was after eight when the couple got home. As usual, she was in a horny mood. He was not, but he had to succumb to her wishes. If he were ever going to remain in her good graces, money wise, he could never say, "Christine, not tonight; I have a toothache."

Lucky for him, she did most of the work. She was a wild thing, roaring and moaning like a lioness caught in a trap. *From where does this woman get her oomph?*

The lovemaking lasted for ten minutes, a history-making record for her.

This woman gives a whole new meaning to biff bam, thank you, sir. Not that he really cared, but the short time she spent doing him was weird and wonderful.

He got up, went downstairs, made that call to the woman and asked if he could come to her home around seven in the morning. She was an early riser and agreed to that time.

It was 6:30 a.m. when Awesome woke up. He showered, dressed and walked into the kitchen. Christine had turned off the percolator.

"Good morning, *ma chérie*. You are up early," he said, patting his wife on her *derrière*.

"And good morning to you, my handsome hunk. Would you like me to pour you a cup of coffee?"

"That is so kind of you, but I have to leave now and check out some wares for the shop. Will you forgive me? I will make it up to you this evening."

"There is nothing to forgive. I will see you tonight. You have a great day." She tongue kissed him and rubbed her body next to his. If he did not have to leave, he would have humped her to eternity.

Awesome took the van and drove to the woman's house, which was stunning from the outside. He went inside and looked around. There were piles of things throughout the four-story house. He wondered how the owner was able to find anything. *To say this woman is a hoarder is putting it mildly.*

He did come across some nice things. There was a crystal pitcher, a sterling silver tea set, an art deco coffee table, a beautiful cedar closet, rare books, artwork, jewelry and other fine furniture. "You do not wish to take any of the items with you when you move?"

"No, I am relocating to another state and will be moving into a studio apartment."

"I see," Awesome said. Just by looking at the pieces, he knew collectors would pay a bundle for some of these items. He called Webster. "Hi, I am sorry to wake you."

"No sweat, I am at the shop."

"I am here at the woman's house and think your friend, *The Collector*, would be interested in some of these bits and pieces."

"Let me give you his number, and mention my name."

He made that call. "Good morning, this is Awesome Petté. Webster Jones referred me to you. I am at a house that has some beautiful antiques, which you may want to look at." *The Collector* was interested, took down the address and would be there in thirty minutes.

"Ma'am, I have someone who will be here shortly to look at some of your possessions."

The Collector arrived with his truck. After close examination, he wanted the closet, books, all of the furniture, the table, and artwork. Whatever he did not want, Awesome would consider buying.

He offered the woman one thousand dollars, which she accepted. He gave Awesome one hundred dollars for calling him and would give Webster one hundred dollars for referring him.

After looking over the other items in her home, Awesome bought the crystal pitcher, the sterling silver tea set, and all the costume jewelry. He gave her two hundred dollars and thanked the woman for her time. She was extremely grateful. "Twelve hundred dollars will go a long way," she said.

Awesome went back to the shop with the merchandise. He displayed the pitcher and the tea set in the window, and the jewelry in the display case.

Webster thanked Awesome for calling *The Collector*. "I made one hundred dollars for referring you. I always get a ten percent referral fee from him."

"I also got one hundred dollars for calling him. We both made out well."

A customer walked into the shop and purchased the pitcher and the tea set for sixty dollars. The day ended on a good note.

Chapter 38

It was Friday, May 23. Since it was a slow morning at the shop, Awesome thought it would be a good time to find a key to open that chest he brought from the woman weeks ago. He knew a locksmith named Ray and gave him a call.

"Hi, Ray, this is Awesome. I have a locked chest that is missing a key."

"What can you tell me about the box?"

"It's a wooden box with intricate patterns and designs and is encrusted with reddish-purple stones. It's the size of a shoebox."

"Can you tell me where it was made?"

"No."

"Are you home or at the shop?"

"I am at the shop."

"I'll be there in twenty minutes."

In less than twenty minutes, Ray was at *Second Hand Treasures*. He looked at the chest. "From where did you get this?"

"I bought it from a homeowner."

Exploring the box very closely, Ray eyes almost popped out of his head; so captivated by the details, he failed to see if any of his keys could open the box. The expression on his face said it all. "How much do you want for this?"

"Oh, it is not for sale. I bought it for my home office." *The way he is studying this chest, there must be more to this box than he is letting on.* "Forget about the key. The box itself is beautiful, and the fact that it cannot be opened will make it even more alluring."

"Well, if you change you mind, give me a call," Ray said, rushing out of the shop.

Awesome took a picture of the chest, called *The Collector*, and e-mailed the image for his assessment.

An hour later, *The Collector* got back to him. "Keep that box in a safe place. I am on my way to Victoria, British Columbia and will return in four weeks."

I was right. Ray knew that chest was valuable and thought he could buy it on the cheap and resell it to the highest bidder. My parents didn't raise any fool.

Awesome had a safe deposit box at another bank. He told Webster he had to leave, would be back in an hour and placed an *out to lunch* sign in the shop's window. He drove to the bank and placed the chest into his safe deposit box.

Upon his return to the shop, Awesome was greeted by another customer. She had a Cartier watch to sell and was asking for two hundred dollars. He knew the watch was worth more, at least fifteen hundred bucks. "I will give you one hundred dollars." She took the money. He decided to keep the watch for himself.

As he was getting ready to go downstairs to chat with Webster, Awesome's cell phone rang. It was Christine reminding him to pick up his tuxedo for tomorrow's reception. With so much on his mind, he almost forgot about the bash.

"Oh, thank you for reminding me."

"My parents are sending a limousine to pick us up at the condominium."

"You have not told them about our home."

"No, I did not think you wanted them to know right away. Remember, you did not want to share our home with anyone until you felt the time was right."

"Yes, I did say that."

"Do you want me to tell them about our estate?"

"Not now, I want to make certain they acknowledge me as your husband and accept me as their son-in-law."

"If they didn't accept you, I don't think they would go out of their way and give us this party."

"They may be doing this to please you."

"I doubt it. My parents would never go this far just to gratify me."

"That remains to be seen," he said. "Christine, a customer just walked in. I'll see you tonight."

Webster was smiling. "Lying to your wife again?"

"She still believes her parents have accepted me."

"When it comes to her mom and dad, she is probably in denial," Webster said. "By the way, one of my associates just called. He still has not come up with any explosive information on the Baileys. Do you want him to keep digging?"

"No, let us wait until after the reception. I want to see what those two are really up to, and what we will need to do to defuse them."

Chapter 39

Awesome and Christine thought it would be better to spend the night at the condominium. They also took some of his clothing to the unit as though they were residing there. They would keep up this pretense until they were ready to announce their true residence.

May 24 turned out to be a bright day. The weather channel predicted temperatures in the mid-sixties. Christine laid out her red silk evening gown with matching shoes and a harmonizing clutch bag. Awesome had a navy blue tuxedo, a red vest and tie, and brown loafers.

As a belated wedding gift, Christine gave Awesome a set of gold cufflinks and a tie clip. It never dawned on him to give her a gift.

"Oh, sweetheart, being so busy, I forgot to buy you something," he said.

"Don't worry. You have already given me so much," she said, caressing his arm.

"Darling, let me make it up to you." He brought her back to bed and made love to her.

"This is the best reward you can ever give me," she said, shouting for joy.

"What time is the limousine coming?" Awesome asked.

"At 2 p.m." It was already 1 p.m.

"Then, it's time for us to get ready." In a flash, they both reached a delightful pinnacle.

The chauffeur arrived on time. The white stretch limousine took up one-quarter of the block. It came with a TV, stereo, and a bar stocked with liquor and snacks. Awesome felt like a superstar. *The Baileys will never go for broke*, he thought.

There was very little traffic on the road. They arrived at *Ocean View Country Club* at 2:55 p.m.

Wow, this is some fancy place. I wonder what the membership fee is. It is probably too rich for my blood. No pun intended.

When the couple entered the club, the Baileys greeted, hugged and kissed their daughter. "As always, you look glamorous; you wear that gown like a monarch," her mother said.

"Why thank you, mother. You also look lovely. Dad, it is nice to see you, looking handsome as always."

"Thank you, Christine."

When it came to Awesome, the Baileys acted as if he were the invisible man. "You and your husband will be sitting at this table; when all the guests arrive, we will declare your marriage," Mary said.

The main room was beyond opulence, accentuated by a beautiful crystal chandelier, art deco designs, parquet floors and spiral stair railings made of 23-carat-gold-leaf.

There was an eight-tiered wedding cake on a decked out table, but there was no groom's cake. On another table were gifts for the bride and groom sent by folks who could not make it to the reception. The third table would exhibit presents from the guests.

Christine noticed how her parents were ignoring Awesome. "You are right. My parents do not like you and will probably never accept you as my husband or into the family."

"Sugar pie, don't worry. I am not offended. It was obvious from the start. Your parents took an instant dislike to me."

"Well, I am upset," she said.

"Let's not allow your parents to spoil this happy occasion."

"You are right. From this point on, it will be you and me against the world."

"Well said," Awesome whispered in Christine's ear.

People were starting to arrive. Christine decided to grab the bull by the horn; she would not allow her parents to humiliate her husband any further. "Awesome, let me introduce you to your future friends and in-laws." She and her husband got up from the table, went into the lobby, and mingled with the crowd.

Christine began introducing her husband to the guests. Her parents were somewhat annoyed but pleased. "This will be the determining moment when we will discover who Mr. Awesome Petté really is," Mary said to her husband.

"Yes, his interaction and body language will give him away," James said in a confident tone.

"It's a pleasure to meet you, Mr. Petté," some said.

"Many happy returns," others pronounced.

Christine's girlfriends from Atlanta were somewhat impressed with her husband. "He is a far cry from that Henry Fuller," one of the females said, sneering.

"Who is Henry Fuller?" Awesome asked with a probing stare.

"He is someone I met while attending college. The relationship did not last. He disappeared without saying a word."

Your meddling parents probably had something do with him vanishing, Awesome thought.

Some guests were trying to get a feel for Awesome. It was obvious to them that he was not from the proper echelon. When people discovered he owned a junk store, they could never see him as one of them.

A few of Christine's relatives were asking "How and where did she meet this fellow?"

"Her husband does not come over as someone with immeasurable wealth," her pompous aunt, from her father's side, uttered.

The rest of the family wanted to know more about his lineage. His name did not appear in any of the social registers; most of the individuals in the Baileys' world never even heard of him.

"How long do you think the marriage will last?" somebody asked.

"Your guess is as good as good as mine," a man replied, laughing.

Christine overheard the snickering and sly remarks made about her husband. It was cruel because these people were associates, close friends and family members making those vicious comments.

The buffet table was breathtaking. A member of the serving staff invited everyone to come to each of the two tables, where hosts served the food into porcelain plates. When guests returned to their tables, they could choose champagne, white or red wine or sparkling water, which would be poured into elegant crystal glasses by attendants.

Everyone was chatting and eating. The Baileys hired an orchestra that played humdrum compositions, a great fit for such a superficial crowd.

As everyone was finishing their meal, the Baileys went on stage. "My husband and I would like to offer our many happy returns to our daughter."

By now, Christine was livid. She got up, went to the pedestal and grabbed the mike from her mother's hand. "You may not like my husband but you could have shown some courtesy for my sake." Tears were rolling down her cheeks. "I married Awesome Petté; that is his name. I did not marry a shadow but a wonderful man who completes me. If you cannot see that, then you no longer have a daughter."

Christine ran off the podium and went back to the table. "Awesome, we are leaving. We do not want to be around people who do not respect us."

The guests gasped. It became quiet. One could not hear a pin drop.

Mary and James Bailey were stunned. "We apologize for our daughter's outburst. The stress of her marriage to that man and this party must have gotten to her. Please continue to enjoy yourselves." They ran after their daughter, but it was too late. Christine and Awesome jumped into the limousine and asked the chauffeur to drive them back to the condominium.

Chapter 40

It was 9:15 p.m. when Awesome and Christine got back to the condominium. Crying, she could not believe how she acted and almost felt awful for her unladylike conduct. She had never displayed such insolence toward her parents. There were times when they got on her last nerve, but it never got to the point where she would reprimand them, especially in public and in front of business associates, friends, and relatives.

Awesome was now ready to put his strategies into motion. He would have more power over Christine and not have to worry about her parents interfering and spoiling everything.

"My precious one, I think we should go back home before your parents come here," he said.

"Awesome, you are right. Let us leave now. I am so happy you did not tell them where we live."

Earlier that day, she parked her car in the garage but was too upset to operate the vehicle. While she waited in the vestibule, Awesome went to retrieve her car. When he drove to the front entrance, she got into the car. They were home in thirty minutes.

"Why don't we go upstairs and talk about what happened," Awesome said, trying to appease Christine. Not that he really cared, because her flare-up worked in his favor.

"Awesome, I don't feel like talking about what took place. We can resume this conversation tomorrow. I am turning in for the night."

"Okay, I will be in my office and will be up soon." As he turned to say goodnight, she was sound asleep.

The next morning, Christine woke up feeling chirpy. She checked her voice mail. There were several messages from her mother. "Christine, why did you go off like that? Your father and I only want the best for you. Please, get back to us."

All of the messages were the same. "Please, call back. We love you. He is going to break your heart." She deleted them all and never wanted to hear from her parents again.

Awesome was in the kitchen; he was drinking papaya juice. Christine came in and kissed him. "Good morning, how did you sleep last night?" he asked.

"I slept like a lamb and have decided to change my cell phone number. Lucky for us, my parents don't have our home phone number."

"Speaking of your parents, they know where the shop is, will stop by and try to get some information as to why we are not at the condominium. What should I tell them?"

"Make up a story."

"I will not have any problems fibbing to your parents," he said with a devilish leer.

Awesome would limit his days at the shop. Instead of conducting business there, he would work from home. He would get one of Webster's buddies to fill in at the shop.

He called Webster but got his voice mail. He usually spent Sundays with his girlfriend, Susan. She would sometimes make him accompany her to church, where the two would repent for all of their sins. "Hey, you will not believe what happened at the reception. I will not be in the shop for the next three days. If you could get one of your pals to take over, I would appreciate it. I'll pay ninety dollars per day." He left instructions to relay to the stand-in employee. "If anyone asks about me or my wife, say, I have no idea when Mr. Petté will be in and have never met his wife."

Until she decides what to do next, Christine would work from home. She went into the garden and connected with her clients online. Over two hundred messages filled her inbox. Most of the posts were from guests wanting to know if she were okay. However, there was one message that disturbed her; she did not know who the sender was, and she could not send a reply:

Mr. Awesome Petté is not who you think he is. You must watch your back.

Guessing the e-mail was from her mother, Christine deleted the post. *You just will not let it go. Why do you always have to pee on the parade? Despite what you or anyone else thinks, I plan to live happily ever after with my husband.*

Faster than termites nibbling on wood, what occurred on May 24, 2008, at *Ocean View Country Club* hit newsstands like a firestorm. Several society newspapers had the following caption:

Daughter of Prominent Family Goes Bananas at Her Wedding Reception

Christine Bailey Petté chastised her parents, in front of guests, for snubbing her husband. She ran out of the club with her spouse. No one has seen or heard from the couple since the confrontation. According to our sources, her husband, Mr. Awesome Petté, is a man of means. He owns a little junk shop in Brooklyn, New York. A spokesperson for the family did not return any of our calls for comments.

Webster called Awesome but got his voice mail. "Congratulations on your fifteen minutes of fame. I can't wait to hear all of the particulars."

When checking his messages, Awesome was confused and could not grasp what Webster was conveying. *What does he mean by your fifteen minutes of fame? What do I have to explain?*

Since he had not been out of the house for three days and had not spoken to anyone, he was unaware as to what was occurring outside of his domain. Christine was spending more time in the garden working on her laptop.

Maybe she knows something.

"Anything new on the Internet?" Awesome asked. He did not want to come over as though he were fishing for some gossip.

"No, I am making arrangements to meet with some of my clients. By the way, I have a new cell phone number. Here it is. Please don't give it to anyone, especially my parents."

"Your number is safe with me." He decided to go to the shop. "Baby, I am going to work. I will see you tonight. Enjoy your day."

"Aren't you forgetting something?" she asked as he was getting ready to leave. She puckered her lips, waiting for him to kiss her.

"I must always remember to lip lock my sugar bun." He gave her a quick kiss and then scurried out of the house.

When Awesome arrived at the shop, Susan was attending to a customer. She looked up and said, "Sir, I'll be with you in one second."

He found how she addressed him very odd. *Why refer to me as sir as though she does not know me.*

When the customer left, Susan said, "Awesome, reporters have been asking a lot of questions about you and your wife and that scene she made at the party."

"Say what! Why would reporters be here and asking questions about my wife?"

"I am assuming you have not read any of the newspapers. What your wife did has been circulating in a few of the neighborhood papers. There were even posts on the Internet about the incident. I have a copy of the rag downstairs. I'll get it for you."

Christine's parents probably came to the shop. Maybe they are monitoring this place, pretending to be reporters, and waiting to pounce on me about the whereabouts of their daughter.

Susan came back and handed the tabloid to him. "You and your wife are celebrities," she said, giggling. "May I have your autograph?" Awesome looked at her as if she were a certified screwball.

"Did anyone come in asking specifically for my wife, Christine?" he asked.

"No, the reporters were only interested in you."

"Well, thank you for taking over the shop."

"It was my pleasure. Here are the receipts for the three days. Will you need me tomorrow?"

"No, I have it covered. If I do need you, I will let Webster know. Here is your pay."

"Thank you, Mr. Petté."

"Don't spend it all in one place."

"I won't." Susan went back downstairs, said goodbye to Webster and left.

Awesome read the piece and wondered how the media obtained this information. *Perhaps there was a reporter at the reception, or maybe her underhanded parents were behind this.*

Chapter 41

Webster came upstairs. "Awesome, you go away for a few days and end up causing a big commotion," he said, laughing. "Is this anyway to get publicity for your business?"

"This is some media hype. The writer neglected to mention the name of the shop."

"No, she didn't. She called it a *little junk shop*." They both cracked up.

"I know Christine's parents were behind this article," Awesome noted. "How else would the media have known where the shop was located?"

"Maybe they were working for the Baileys. Nevertheless, my associates still have not found any damaging information on them. We will have to get together and come up with some salacious news on them and at the same time use the information to our benefit."

"We will meet at my house. My wife's parents will move heaven and earth to find their daughter. Presently, they do not know where we live. They believe we are residing at the condominium. Whenever I come and leave the shop, I will always use the back entrance in case I am being watched or followed," Awesome said.

"That's a good idea," Webster responded. "I also think you should have someone else manage the shop until this news broadcast blows over."

"You mean someone like Susan?" Awesome asked with a wink.

"No, in a couple of months, she is going back to California to attend college."

"Oh, how nice," Awesome said.

"I can find someone else to fill in for you, Webster said."

"Good, I will offer the same pay per day."

Webster had a cousin who would be perfect for the job. She was a former manager at a high-end hair salon until it went belly-up. He gave her a call, explaining what the job would involve and what the pay would be, but it would only be a temporary position. If interested, she could come in for an interview. She was interested.

Awesome agreed to see Webster's cousin. Rather than come to the shop, he had her come to the house. Her name was Amy Washington. She was sixty years old but could pass for twenty-five and would be the right fit for the shop. She was sophisticated and articulate. In addition, she was good at following orders and keeping secrets.

Amy had an appointment to see Awesome on Sunday at ten in the morning. He never told Christine about the interview or that he was thinking of hiring a short-term manager for the shop. When the doorbell rang, she went to answer and was surprised to see this beautiful woman standing there. "Good morning, I have an appointment with Mr. Petté."

Hearing Amy's voice, Awesome rushed to the door and nudged Christine to the side. "It is nice to see you. Please, come in." He steered Amy to the living room, never introducing her to his wife.

The two went into the office; he shut the door and explained everything to Amy. If the Baileys ever came into the shop, she knew exactly what to say and what not to say when it came to him and his wife. She also understood the shop was a front for Webster's illegal enterprise.

Amy received a key to the shop and would report to work on Monday. Awesome would have someone deliver merchandise to the store when needed. If there were any problems, Webster would be there to help. The plan was slowly falling into place.

After Amy left, Christine approached Awesome and asked, "Who was that woman?"

"She is going to manage the shop for a while. I am taking the next several months off." He never mentioned how Christine's outburst at the party appeared in some of the local newspapers and that a few reporters came to the shop, trying to get more information about him.

"You did not tell me you were planning to take a sabbatical."

"At the last minute, I thought it would be nice for us to spend more time together, or maybe take that long awaited honeymoon and get your mind off of the reception and your parents."

"That sounds lovely, but I have made some plans for the next couple of months, which involve traveling. A couple of my clients need assistance with their companies, so the honeymoon will have to wait."

Good. This gives me more time to work on my scheme. Happy trails to you. "Oh, baby, that is too bad. I was looking forward to spending more quality time with you. As always, the business must come first," he said with an insincere grin.

"When you make love to me, it's like being on a honeymoon." When she made that statement, the doorbell rang. "I'll get it," she said. When she went to the door, a messenger, who looked like Sasquatch, had a packet that required her husband's signature. "I can sign for it," she said, feeling uneasy.

"I am sorry, but only Mr. Awesome Petté can sign for this. If he is not home, I will have to re-deliver the package?"

"Who is it, Christine?" Awesome shouted.

"It's a package for you, and you have to sign for it."

He came to the door, signed for the item and got a receipt. Awesome went to his office, closed the door and opened the parcel. When he read the content, he shouted, "Whoopee...!" The commotion went on for almost five minutes.

Christine did not hear his joyful outburst. His office was well insulated. Yet, she could not get over that courier, who almost scared the bejesus out of her.

Awesome was beside himself. That packet contained information on the chest he purchased from the homeowner in Stuyvesant Heights. Unfortunately for her, she was unaware of its real value.

According to *The Collector*, the image Awesome sent to him was a dead ringer of a chest published in a collectors' magazine back in 1990. The box itself was not worth a penny, but the embedded stones were.

The original owner was a Ghanaian bank magnate, who was divorcing his wife in 1989. To hide the gemstones, so his wife could not get them as part of a divorce settlement, he cemented the gems into the chest and shipped it to a friend, who was living in New York, for safe keeping.

The magistrate finalized the divorce on February 15, 1990. The owner had the box shipped back to him, but supposedly, the chest was either lost or stolen during transport.

The tycoon placed an ad in a catalog, which was distributed worldwide to millions of collectors; he described the chest as a family heirloom. Anyone who could locate the box would receive a generous reward, but on March 5, 1990, the proprietor died under mysterious circumstances. Ultimately, the box became a distant memory until it showed up in Awesome's shop.

Awesome had questions and thought about the woman who sold him the chest. *Was her husband the friend who received the box and decided to keep it? Did he know the importance of the box, hid it but died before he could tell his wife about its worth?*

Calling the woman now and asking about her husband would suggest he might have been keeping secrets from her. Besides, she was gone, and new owners were now occupying the house. He also wondered if the house had additional treasures hidden in plain sight.

That was water under the bridge. Awesome was now the rightful owner, and if the stones were authentic, he would be the one to set the price for those jewels.

Chapter 42

The Collector returned from his trip and immediately called Awesome. "I would like to meet with you and examine that chest. If it is the real deal, you stand to make a lot of money."

Awesome asked *The Collector* to meet him at the bank. The last place to hold a meeting was at his house. He did not know *The Collector* that well, even though he was an associate of Webster. He wanted to be on the safe side. Until he was sure about the stones' value, he would keep that box in the bank's vault.

The two agreed to meet Friday morning at 9 a.m. *The Collector* was waiting when Awesome arrived. They went into the bank and downstairs to the basement. The bank officer, with a key, opened the safe, removed a secured container, placed it on the table and left.

Awesome opened the container with his key and removed the chest. *The Collector* examined the stones and said, "You hit the jackpot. I know someone who would be willing to pay you 2.5 million dollars for these stones."

"Make it three million, and you have a deal." Awesome knew the stones appreciated over time. In 1990, the stones were worth two million. Eighteen years later, they would be worth more. *If this buyer really wants these trinkets, he will pay my asking price.*

"I have to make a call," *The Collector* said. He quoted Awesome's asking price to the person on the other end. When he got off the phone, he asked, "Where should I wire the money?" He gave him his offshore bank account number. In a flash, Awesome was three million dollars richer.

The Collector removed the stones and placed them into a blue velvet pouch. "Mr. Petté, it was a pleasure doing business with you."

"Likewise," Awesome said.

The two men left the bank and went their separate ways. Awesome purchased bogus stones, which resembled the real ones. When he got home, he cemented the ornaments on the box with *Crazy Glue* and hid the chest in a safe place. He would give the box to his wife as a final going away, birthday, Christmas, and Kwanzaa gift, killing one bird with four stones.

Chapter 43

Awesome made arrangements for Webster and his contact to meet at the house. The details they selected to use against the Baileys would not only destroy them but would also have a devastating impact on Christine.

"I will have to move the money from our joint account before we release this information," Awesome said. "So we will have to weigh everything before we make our final move."

"Have you decided which offshore account you will wire the money into?" Webster asked.

"It will probably be the Caymans."

Just like Webster, Awesome had an account there but under a pseudo name. Webster also knew how to hack into bank accounts, withdraw money and wire the funds through various paths, eventually landing into an untraceable special account.

Law enforcement and banking officials would never detect the unlawful transactions. It would be as though the person never had an account at the depository.

"When I am done with the Baileys, it will be too late for them to do anything to me. They will be too busy digging themselves out of the hole we have created and looking over their shoulders," Awesome predicted.

Webster and his pal were finished conducting their business. As they were getting ready to leave, Christine was parking her car.

"Awesome, your wife just drove into the driveway," Webster said.

"Come back here and go into the office. When I take her upstairs, I will keep her occupied. Leave as quietly as you can."

Before Christine could put the key into the lock, Awesome opened the door. "I am so glad you are home. I missed you." He picked up her, carried her upstairs and into the bedroom.

She was hot and ready. They removed their clothing and jumped into bed. He got on top her and jammed his head inside of her. She screamed, "Mercy, mercy. Spank me baby; amuse me."

He shouted, "Yes, baby, I am coming."

Meanwhile, Webster and his friend, hearing the couple's cries of ecstasy, hurried out of the house, dashed into their cars and took off, each wishing they had captured that episode on their cell phone.

Chapter 44

It was now mid-July, and the Baileys had not heard from their daughter. No one knew where Christine was. Her girlfriends in Atlanta had not heard from her. She was not replying to her e-mails, and her cell phone number was no longer in service.

On several occasions, her mother went to the condominium; finally, the doorman said, "Your daughter has not been here since she left with a man on May 24."

"You mean that so-called spouse of hers." The employee had no idea the man was her husband.

James decided to go to the shop to confront his daughter's husband. Instead, Amy greeted him. "Mr. Petté is out of the country and left me in charge."

"When will he be back?" James asked in an angry tone.

"I do not know. If you like, you can leave your name and number, and when he gets back, I will have him call you."

"Do you know if his wife is with him? I am her father."

"I am sorry; I never met the owner's wife and do not know if she is with him. As I mentioned…"

"Ah, forget it. If I do not hear from either one of them by the end of this week, I will call the police and report my daughter missing. You can pass that on to your boss," James said, leaving the shop and slamming the door behind him.

Amy called Awesome and gave him the useful details about James Bailey asking about him and his wife and threatening to report his daughter missing. "Don't worry, I have it covered. You are doing a grand job. Thank you, Ms. Washington."

"You are welcome, Mr. Petté."

Christine was out of town on business and would not return until July 31. He got in touch with her. "Your father went to the shop looking for you. If he does not hear from you by the end of this week, he will go to the police and file a missing persons report."

"I would call my parents but I don't want them to know my new number."

"You can place a block on your phone."

"Like that is going to stop them from finding me."

"Buy a throwaway cell phone. No one will be able to track your calls."

"Just so happens, I am in a shopping mall and see a mobile kiosk, which sells disposable cell phones. So I will purchase one now."

"Good, when you reach your folks, let me know."

"I will. I love you."

"Love you back," he said, smiling.

Christine purchased a disposable phone. She dreaded making that call but did. Her mother answered. "I hear you are planning to send the bloodhounds after me. If I want you to know where I am, I would tell you. Please understand that I am cutting you and dad out of my life."

"How can you be so insolent?" Her mother then heard a click. "Christine! Christine!" Her mother tried to call back, but there was no dial tone.

James walked in. "Who was that on the phone?"

"It was your daughter."

"Oh, now she's my daughter. Where is she?"

"I don't know. She made it very clear that we are no longer her parents."

"Christine does not mean that. She is upset. Eventually, she will come around when she discovers who that Awesome really is. Did you call her back?"

"Her number did not show. I tried redialing but nothing happened. I truly believe that man has brainwashed our child. She would never treat us in such a deplorable manner," Mary said.

"Love is blind," James said.

"Well, this is war. Mr. Awesome Petté messed with the wrong people."

That evening, Christine contacted Awesome. "I called my mother and made it very clear that she and my dad are no longer a part of my life. As far as I am concerned, I no longer have parents."

"Honey, I am so sorry it came to this. I was hoping they would come around, but I guess it was never meant to be."

"It does not matter. We have each other, and that is all that matters."

"My Christine, we will always be there for each other."

"Awesome, I will see you in two weeks."

Chapter 45

The Baileys were not going to allow Awesome to be in control when it came to their daughter's well-being. They called Danny Mayo. He came to their office. "We want you to find Christine and bring her back home."

"Is she missing?" Danny asked.

"As far as we know that man is hiding her somewhere."

"What man?"

"Awesome Petté, who on earth would I be talking about," Mary responded, showing her indignation toward Danny for asking such a dim-witted question.

"Oh, you mean her husband. When was the last time you spoke to her?"

"She called a couple of weeks ago and said we were no longer her parents. When I tried to call her back, there was no service."

"Most likely, she used a burner phone. You must understand your daughter is an adult and a married woman. If she does not want to have anything to do with you, what can I do? I cannot force her to leave her husband unless he poses an imminent threat to her. From what I can see, she is not in any danger."

"Listen, are you going to find her, or do we need to hire someone else to do the job?" a furious Mary asked.

If you want to throw good money after bad, heck, I will take the job. "I will start by questioning her husband at his shop."

"Don't waste your time," James interjected. "I went there; he is out of the country. The person managing the place would not give me any information on his whereabouts."

"Well, wherever he is, I'll find him. Where does the couple live?"

"They live in our condominium, but the doorman has not seen them since May 24."

"I'll get on it right away, but I cannot make any promises."

Danny went straight to *Second Hand Treasures* and spoke to Amy Washington. He knew right from the start that he was not going to get much out of her. Frankly speaking, he did not give a rat's behind if Christine never wanted to see her parents. He never liked the Baileys, did not know anything about Awesome, but if he made her happy, her parents should be jumping through hoops.

Amy made that call. "Mr. Petté, a Danny Mayo was here; he was asking questions about you and your wife. Of course, I told him nothing."

"My wife's parents have a chip in the brain. Christine wants nothing to do with them. When are they going to wake up and smell the coffee?"

"Is there anything I can do, Mr. Petté?" Amy asked.

"No, the day of reckoning is about to fall on them. Nevertheless, thank you for all you have done; if anyone else shows up, continue the same routine."

"I will keep you posted of any new developments. Have a nice evening."

"You do the same."

Danny wanted to keep the Baileys on pins and needles. Three days later, he went online to see if Christine had booked a flight. Bingo! She flew to Washington, D.C. He sent her an e-mail explaining her parents had hired him to find her. *I want nothing to do with those two* was her reply.

Her message was loud and clear. That evening, he contacted the Baileys and met with them the next day. "Your daughter and her husband did not book any flights. They could be anywhere, but their location is not showing up on any of my searches. If you want me to continue looking, I will."

"Shelve it until further notice. When our daughter is ready to come home, we will welcome her with open arms," James said.

"No, I want him to continue looking for our daughter. Who knows what that man is doing to her," Mary ordered.

"Mary, let it go. Mr. Mayo, how much do we owe you?"

"Five hundred dollars."

"Are you kidding? You are charging that much for doing nothing," Mary yelled with fire in her eyes.

Mr. Bailey paid Danny with cash. "Thank you for your service."

"Thank you, Mr. Bailey. If I can be of additional assistance, call me."

"Don't hold your breath," Mary shrieked.

"Mary, please…" James pleaded.

"Mr. Mayo, you are no longer on our payroll," Mary said, demanding that he show himself out of the office.

As if I really give a damn.

Chapter 46

Christine finished her business in D.C. earlier than she had anticipated. It was Friday evening when she walked into the house. She was ready to jump into Awesome's arms and make love to him, but he was not home.

She went upstairs, unpacked, showered and got into her new sexy lingerie, which she purchased at an upscale boutique; she went straight to bed and waited for him.

Suddenly, the home phone rang. "You are in great danger," the caller said.

"Who is this?" There was silence on the other end. Ten minutes later, the phone rang again. "Hello."

"Awesome Petté is a deceitful person; he will break your heart."

"Why do you keep calling?" There was a click. At first, Christine thought it was her mother but remembered she never gave her the home phone number.

Even if her mother knew where they lived and looked up the number in the telephone book or called directory assistance, it would be futile because the number was unlisted.

It was probably a prankster, Christine thought.

The landline phone was old school; there was no way the caller's number would show. There was no redial button, so Christine would never know who made that call.

It was after eight when Awesome arrived home. He went up to the bedroom and could not believe his eyes.

"It's good to see you. I thought you were coming home next week." *Good thing I did not have a woman with me.*

"My work with the client finished ahead of schedule. The company loved my presentation and did not see the need for me to stay any longer. Besides, I missed you; come to momma."

This woman is going to be the death of me.

"I missed you too. Give me a couple of minutes to get myself together." Knocking boots was the last thing on his mind. He took a shower and returned all dried.

"Oh, baby, you should have let the water run down on your searing body. It turns me on," she purred.

"If you like, I can go back and shower my body with warm water and return dripping wet."

"Stop it and do me as though we are participating in a lovemaking marathon."

"Yes, your highness; now open wide." He surged inside of her, releasing hot lava throughout her sensuous channel.

"Sweetie, you are outdoing yourself."

"Thank you, ma'am, I am here to please you." They stimulated each other for several hours until they both fell asleep.

Awesome woke up around 9:30 a.m. His cell phone was ringing. He went downstairs to answer the call. It was Webster. "Good morning, hope I did not wake you. We are having a going away party for Susan. Why don't you join us at our usual meeting place at 6 p.m.?"

"I was up all night and only got a couple hours of snooze."

"What were you doing?"

"I was hitting several home runs."

"Who was the lucky lady?"

"It was my wife."

"Wait a minute. I thought she wasn't due back until next week."

"As luck would have it, her meeting was a hit, so she did not have to stay. Imagine my surprise when I saw her in bed, looking and acting like a strumpet and ready to have her flower plucked."

"I understand why you were up all night. No pun intended," Webster said, snickering.

"I will have to miss that event but give my best wishes to Susan."

"I will. Take care."

Chapter 47

Awesome had a lot on his plate. It was now September. He was planning to leave, for good, sometime in December. Conducting meetings in his home office would be ideal.

The room is soundless, and Christine would not be able to eavesdrop on our conversations, not that she would, but one can never be too guarded.

The first meeting was this evening, but he never mentioned it to his wife. Only Webster and Boris would attend.

Christine was upstairs when she heard the doorbell ring. Standing at the edge of the stairs, she saw her husband greeting two men in the foyer. He was careful not to address them by their names.

As she started to walk down the stairs, one of the men signaled him to look up. "There is no need for you to come down. This is a business meeting, which should not last more than an hour," Awesome said.

Even though she was a silent partner, she was not too keen having strangers coming to the house for meetings.

He could use the apartment in the shop to meet with clients. I will have to talk to him about that.

Awesome and his cohorts went over the fabricated chronicle about the Baileys. They decided releasing the particulars to the media, anonymously, would be best. Not only would they send the information to the printed media but would also broadcast it on the World Wide Web.

Webster was in charge of getting an untraceable e-mail address to dispense the content to thousands of sites, magazines, and blogs. He would also structure deeds to properties, which would include fake titleholders.

"This is the first phase. Our next meeting will be in October. Any news that you come across should be sent by messenger to me," Awesome said.

"You got it," Boris replied.

"Sure thing, boss," Webster said. The meeting was over, and the men left.

Awesome went upstairs to check on Christine. She was reading a fashion magazine, whose editor was a friend of hers. "How did your meeting go?"

"It was very productive." That is all he would say.

"I do have a suggestion. You can conduct your meetings at the apartment over the shop. Unless you know these people personally, you must be very careful inviting strangers into our home."

"I would, but you never know who is scrutinizing the shop. Your parents may have spies watching and following me. The next thing you know, your mom and dad are standing in front of our doorway, trying to force you to leave me."

"Oh my, I never thought of that. You are right to hold your meetings here. What was I thinking?"

"Your parents are very resourceful and probably have connections throughout the city. All it takes is for one individual to discover where we live, and we are history."

"Relentlessly, you are two steps ahead of my parents."

"I have to be, my love."

Chapter 48

Mary Bailey was beside herself. Anyone who got in her way would face her rage, including James. No longer was she going to take her husband's advice and wait for Christine to come to her senses. Without discussing it with him, she hired another private eye to find her daughter. An old friend recommended him. The investigator's name was John Shaw.

John always wanted to be a policeman, but he scored low on the written exam and failed the physical component, so he took an online course: *Applying Unique Methods in Investigative Work.*

After completing the module, he received a certificate and purchased high-tech tools that enabled him to find anything or anyone.

He had a laptop with high-speed Internet, infrared cameras, recording devices concealed in jewelry, pens, and eyeglasses, and mobile devices with Global Positioning System. He did not have any successful cases to speak of, which is why he had so much time on his hands.

For all purposes, John was no Danny Mayo. He had been in business for one year and had two cases to his name.

His first assignment was locating a missing three-legged Siamese cat. An animal shelter found her and notified the owner, who demanded his deposit back since John failed to find the two thousand dollars pure-bred feline.

The second job involved following a most likely cheating husband. The wife suspected he was sleeping with his secretary. John took pictures of the husband going into a hotel with a young woman, whom he thought was the husband's mistress, but she turned out to be the wife. From that day on, people would refer to him as the *bumbling private eye*.

He thought finding Christine was going to be a walk in the park. Mary gave him all the information on Awesome

Petté and a one thousand dollar retainer. "I want quick results. Do I make myself clear?"

"Yes, Mrs. Bailey; give me one week. I will find your daughter and bring her back to you."

The only information John had was the address to the shop and condominium, a photo of Christine and her husband, and Danny Mayo's report on Awesome.

For three days, John staked out the condominium. There were no signs of Christine or her husband. He offered to pay the doorman to call him when the couple showed, but the employee refused the money and said, "Sir, please leave the premises, or I will call security."

John's next stop was the shop. From his car, he saw customers coming and going but no sign of Awesome or Christine. He went inside to question Amy, but she gave him the same answers as she gave to others who came seeking the couple's location.

One week passed. Mary demanded a progress report from John. "I am still working on it," he said.

"Work harder or I'll find someone else to take on the job."

After trying various avenues, finding Christine was turning out to be harder than John had anticipated. After working on the case for two weeks, he was no closer to finding his client's daughter. He made that dreaded call. "Mrs. Bailey, I am not having any luck pinpointing your daughter."

"What kind of investigator are you?"

"I have tried every angle imaginable. Since I don't have much to go on, there is nothing more I can do for you."

"Oh, I beg to differ, Mr. Shaw. You will give me back my deposit, or I will make certain you never work in this state again. Do I make myself clear?"

He was well aware of her power, ruining people at the drop of a hatpin. Moreover, he neglected to have her sign a contract that would have protected him from returning her deposit and folded like a cheap suit. "I will refund all of your money."

"I expect to see you in my office with the cash tomorrow at 10 a.m. And don't be late."

The next morning, John arrived thirty minutes late with the cash. "Mrs. Bailey, I am sorry I could not fulfill my obligation."

One week later, law enforcement closed John Shaw's agency for operating without a license; he also had to pay a ten thousand dollar fine.

Chapter 49

It was mid-October. Awesome had another meeting with Webster and Boris. "Webster, it is time for you to be Manny Smith again."

"Good, what do you want me to do?"

"Contact the Baileys. Tell them you wish to buy some properties from them. We need to take their mind off Christine for a while. What better way to distract them by throwing bogus money their way. Of course, this will be done on the Internet."

"Consider it done. I will send an e-mail and ask them to send pictures of the homes they have for sale, which they think they own but don't," Webster said, laughing.

"Boris, do all the papers look realistic," Awesome asked.

"Yes, Webster did such an excellent job; these documents are going to fool the most seasoned individual. I would never question their authenticity because they look so real."

"Good, we will proceed and meet here next month."

Christine was upstairs. She heard the men leave and went to the window to get a good look at their faces but it was too dark outside; for some reason, the streetlights never came on.

Awesome came upstairs and said nothing to his wife.

"I see you had company," Christine said. He never answered her. Suddenly, the phone rang. She answered, "Good evening."

"You must take my warnings seriously. Mr. Awesome Petté does not love you," the voice on the other end said. Christine hung up.

"Who was that?" Awesome asked.

"Probably someone my parents hired to harass us."

"What did the person say?"

"It is not worth mentioning."

Awesome kissed her on the forehead, went downstairs and pranced into his office. *Things are really looking up.*

Webster/Manny Smith sent an e-mail to the Baileys:

October 15, 2008

Dear Mr. and Mrs. Bailey:

We met at Second Hand Treasures on its opening day. We had dinner at that lovely restaurant across the street from the shop. I told you my parents own an auction company in Barbados.

I am looking to purchase a brownstone in Brooklyn. Money is no object. A two or four family residence would be ideal since I plan to use the house as a rental property and want you to be the managing agent.

Coming to New York now would not be possible, but if you could e-mail me some listings along with photos of the homes, I would be indebted to you.

I can provide you with a letter of credit from my three banks and other references for your review.

Looking forward to hearing from you. I remain,
Best regards,
Manny Smith

He called Awesome. "I e-mailed what we discussed to the Baileys. When we meet Sunday, I will bring a copy of that message."

"Perfect, I will see you then."

Christine was in the garden reading a society newspaper. "What's the latest news?" Awesome asked.

"Someone I know is getting married next week. The bride and I grew up together. Her father is a cultural attaché at the United Nations, and her mother is a stockbroker at a major brokerage house."

"That is nice. Let us hope your friend has better luck than I did when your parents found out we were married," he said.

"I am sure both families are thrilled. The bride and groom are gynecologists and have their own practice in a building, which my parents own."

"Well, the couple can amuse each other during office hours," Awesome said, laughing aloud.

"That was funny. You just stimulated by libido. Let us do it now. You be the doctor. I will be the patient."

There I go again with my big mouth. He was not in the mood for sex but had no choice. He was too close to getting what he wanted from her. "Okay, Mrs. Petté, move your body to the edge of the bed and spread your legs wide."

"Yes, *Doctor Feel Good*," she said.

Christine had him doing cartwheels and calisthenics. When Awesome woke up, his body was aching. He could barely move.

"Good morning, *Mr. Good and Plenty*. You were like a tiger in my vessel, getting down and dirty. How do you maintain such stamina," she asked.

"I guess you bring out the lust in me," he replied. "How on earth did we get down here?" It was as though she had hexed him to the point where he could not remember what occurred or how he got to where he was.

"It's my little secret," she answered with a devilish sneer.

He never wanted to find himself in such a state, not remembering how he landed in the basement. He had to be in complete control if his plot was going to work.

What is she up to? Does she suspect anything? Is she trying to throw me off my game? There cannot be any slip-ups. I have come too far for this plan to fail.

Christine went upstairs, leaving Awesome alone. After remaining there for thirty minutes, he got up and went upstairs to the bedroom. He searched high and low for clues that might help him understand last night's events.

Then it dawned on him. *That heifer must have drugged me.*

As he went to check inside the pillowcase, a small plastic bag fell to the floor. He finally got it; she was giving him sex enhancement supplements.

How long has she been doing this? Did she take any of these capsules too? Awesome wondered.

He sat on the bed contemplating his next move.

Should I approach her about what I discovered, remain silent or replace these pills with placebos? He decided on the latter. There were ten capsules remaining.

While Christine was in the living room reading a book, he went into the kitchen, opened each capsule, and replaced the powder with baking soda.

It was now time for Awesome to speed up his tactics. He called Webster and told him what had happened. "And here you thought you were the sex apparatus, leading her down the erotica road," Webster said, cheering him on.

"She is devious," Awesome said.

"Now you know. When do you want to meet?"

"Can you come over tomorrow evening around six? I will explain what I want you to do.

"Six o'clock works for me."

Chapter 50

Christine was preparing dinner when the doorbell rang. She was about to see who it was, but Awesome beat her to the punch.

"Hi, I have the information you requested, Mr. Petté," Webster said. Whenever he came to the house, he never said his name.

"Come in, sir," Awesome replied.

Christine came into the foyer but she could not see Webster's features. He sported a hoodie, covered his face with a scarf and had on sunglasses. She found this peculiar since it was not cold, and it was nighttime. *Why is he wearing shades?*

"Good evening, sir," she said. Webster never answered her. He and Awesome went straight into the office and closed the door.

Christine went back into the kitchen. She was hoping the stranger would stay for dinner, so she could get to meet him. She tapped on the office door.

"What is it?" an irritated Awesome asked.

"Is the gentleman staying for dinner? I can set an extra plate."

"No. Thank you for asking."

"Your wife is the merry housewife," Webster said.

"And she is a nosey one at that, so I want to scare the living daylights out of her and keep her occupied. This way she won't have time to meddle in our affairs."

"Before I forget, here is a copy of the e-mail I sent to the Baileys."

Awesome read the message. "This is fantastic. We will see how long it takes for them to respond."

"So how do you want me to put the fear of God into your wife?"

"I am taking my wife out to dinner on Halloween. I want you to ransack my office. Here is the key to the house. I will leave a Cartier watch, some cash, and gold coins in my desk draw. Leave the draw open, but don't remove the items."

"That should be fun. I will park across the street. When I see you and your wife leave, I will wait fifteen minutes and make certain the coast is clear before I enter your home. What time do you plan to leave?"

"At 7:30 p.m. The restaurant is having a party. We should return home after midnight."

"If there is nothing else, I will leave."

"I think that is all for now. If anything new turns up, I will give you a call."

Webster quietly left the house, got into his car and drove off. Christine never heard the visitor leave. She heard Awesome come out of his office. "Honey, dinner is ready."

"I'll be there in a minute."

Just as Christine was placing the food on the table, the phone rang. "Hello, hello, hello. Who is this? Why do you keep calling and leaving such messages?"

"I am trying to help you. Your husband will hurt you in the long run."

"I know my parents put you up to this. You might as well give up. I will never leave my husband." The caller hung up.

"Who were you talking to?" Awesome asked.

"Again, it was that prankster calling. If this keeps up, we should think about changing our home number."

"I have a customer who used to work for the telephone company. Maybe he can trace the call. It is probably some kid fooling around. Do not let it get to you. Let's sit down and eat."

"You are probably right. Please talk to him and see what he can do."

"I will call him tomorrow."

"Do I know this person?" she asked.

"I doubt it. He does not get out much and sends his personal assistant to buy items from the shop."

"Oh, I see."

Chapter 51

The Baileys were happy to hear from Manny Smith, especially Mary. She had a couple of properties to show. One was a two family brownstone; the other was a four family Victorian. Both homes were located in Fort Greene, Brooklyn. The brownstone was selling for $875,000; the Victorian was going for two million dollars.

Mary would handle everything and sent a video of the two homes and a documentary on Fort Greene, which highlighted its people, the movers and the shakers, businesses, social activities, beautiful tree line streets and exquisite homes. She was looking forward to assisting Mr. Smith.

Webster received the video and replied to Mary's message:

October 28, 2008

Dear Mrs. Bailey:

Thank you for your quick reply and for the videos. I will review the clips and decide which home to buy.

You will hear from me soon with my decision. Give my regards to your husband. I remain,
Very truly yours,
Manny Smith

Webster called Awesome. "I heard from the Baileys. Mary sent me two videos, which I want you to see. Can I come over this evening?"

"Sure. Christine is home; make certain you hide your face."

It was 8 p.m. when Webster arrived. Awesome saw him parking his car and went downstairs to let him in. Christine was watching TV, so she never heard what was going on downstairs.

"She is upstairs. Let's hurry into the office before she comes down," Awesome whispered.

Webster brought his laptop, where the videos were stored. Awesome watched the clips and was very impressed. "Which house should I buy?" Webster asked.

"Buy both."

"I knew you would say that. You really want to suck it to the Baileys."

"And the best is yet to come," Awesome declared.

"I will contact Mary Bailey on November 7. I don't want to come over as too anxious."

"Good. And all the papers are in order?"

"Yes. Boris went over the letter of credit for each of the banks in Africa and the Caribbean. I have bogus references and credit reports."

"The next item on the agenda is to examine all the properties that the Baileys have for sale. I believe the last count was six, which includes the two you will pretend to buy." Awesome said. "Does Boris have the addresses of all the properties in the couple's name?"

"Yes."

"Excellent. We will remove the Baileys' names as the titleholders and replace them with fake names. If I recall, the couple owns sixty-two properties."

"That sounds about right, but I will have to confirm the count with Boris since he is the one with all of the deeds."

"Okay, all assignments should be completed by the end of November."

The meeting ended at 9 p.m. Christine was wondering what Awesome was doing. She got out of bed and was about to go downstairs; suddenly, she saw Awesome talking to someone. She could not make out what they were saying, never saw the person's face and wondered why she did not hear the doorbell ring.

Earlier, she saw her husband looking out the window; then, he went downstairs.

Who was that person? Awesome did not tell me he was having company. Lately, he has been very secretive with his business meetings.

Awesome walked into the bedroom. "Honey, I did not know you were awake?"

"I heard you talking to someone and was about to come downstairs," Christine said.

He had to think fast. "Oh, it was a wholesaler; he was attempting to sell me some antiques. I saw him from the window and went to let him in before he could ring the bell. I did not want to disturb you."

"It is okay. I know how busy you are when it comes to the shop."

"With the holidays approaching, this will be the busiest time of the year," he said.

"When do you plan to go back to the shop?" she asked.

"I am thinking about going back after the New Year."

Chapter 52

It was Halloween. Awesome was getting ready to take Christine to one of their favorite restaurants in DUMBO. Webster parked his car in front of the house, waiting for the couple to leave. It was 7:30 p.m. when they departed.

Webster waited fifteen minutes. As he was about to get out of his car, he saw an individual casing the house. At first, he thought it was a kid attempting to play trick or treat, but the person never rang the doorbell. Instead, he opened the door with a key and went inside.

What is going on here? Where did that person come from?

Immediately, he called Awesome but got his voice mail. He did not want to leave a message, fearing his wife might inadvertently pick up the cell phone and listen to the message.

With his cell phone, he would snap a picture of the person coming out of the house. Twenty minutes later, the man came out and started walking. Webster got out of his car and followed him for two blocks. The man got into a truck. On the side of the van was a sign that read *Ray's Locksmith Service*. Webster took a picture of the truck.

I know that name; why would he break into Awesome's house, and what was he looking for? Webster decided not to go back to the house. Instead, he would go home and try to reach Awesome later or tomorrow morning.

When Awesome and Christine arrived home, it was one o'clock in the morning. "I must go into the office and check on something. I'll be right up." When he walked into the room, he smiled, and in a pretentious voice yelled, "No! No!"

Hearing her husband's distraught voice, Christine ran downstairs to check. When she entered the office, what she saw shook her to the core. Files, folders, papers, and desk drawers were scattered all over the place. "Who on earth did this?" she asked.

"It looks like someone broke into our home but was only searching for something in this office."

"I am calling the police," Christine said. She did not want to use the home phone; she felt the intruder might have left fingerprints on the handset. When she removed her cell phone from her bag, Awesome snatched the device out of her hand.

"There is no need to call the police. As far as I can see, nothing is missing. It was probably some kids playing a Halloween gag."

"But how did they get in. The lock was not broken, and the windows were not shattered."

"If someone wants to get into a home, they will find a way without force. Maybe they found the spare key under the doormat."

What spare key. "I never knew there was a spare key under the doormat," a baffled Christine said.

"I must have forgotten to tell you. My parents kept one under there because my father would always lose his house keys."

"Let me help you straighten up."

"That is not necessary. You go to bed. I'll be up before you know it," an annoyed Awesome said.

Christine was frightened. To think someone would have the audacity to break into the house had her nerves on edge. This is why she did not like Awesome meeting with strangers in their home. Maybe the visitor, whose face she never saw, broke into the house and rummaged through the office.

Even more eerie was one of the drawers tossed on the floor held an expensive watch, gold coins, and cash. One had to be blind as a bat not to have seen those items.

When Awesome came into the bedroom, Christine felt a little better but wondered if the thief was still in the house, hiding somewhere in the basement. "Did you check the cellar?"

"Check the cellar for what," he asked.

"To make certain no one is hiding there."

"Don't be ridiculous. The intruder is long gone."

"Maybe we should think about getting an alarm system."

"I was thinking the same thing. We will talk more about it tomorrow. Now go to sleep."

Christine was not as composed as Awesome was. She still had a sensation that someone was still in the house, but she and Awesome finally fell asleep.

Awesome called Webster. "Thank you for a job well done."

"Don't thank me. You need to thank Ray, the locksmith."

"Say what! I should be thanking who?"

"I tried calling you last night, but your phone went to voice mail. I did not want to leave a message, fearing your wife might check your incoming calls. As I was getting ready to get out of my car, I saw someone going into your house. I waited for the individual to leave and followed him. He got into a van, which read *Ray's Locksmith Service*. I even took a picture of him and the van."

"I knew Ray was up to no good when he saw that chest. I had called him to unlock it because there was no key. He wanted to buy the box from me, but I said it was for my home office."

"Why would he want to steal a chest?"

"It was not the chest he wanted; it was the stones embedded in the box that he was after. He realized they were worth something, but at that time, he did not know how much. He must have just found out and thought he would break into my house and steal the box."

"Did he find the box?"

"No, I hid it out of harm's way."

"Good thinking," Webster said.

Ray was someone his parents would use regularly when they had locks installed in the house. His parents were thinking about renting out rooms to earn extra money. After hearing some of the horror stories that many homeowners went through when it came to deadbeat tenants, they decided against it.

It was understandable how Ray got into the house so easily. He had keys to the house and could come and go as he pleased if warranted.

Since he did not find the box on the first go-round, Awesome thought, *he may attempt to come back, and if he does, he will get the shock of his life.*

Christine returned home from a long jog, which she always found soothing. Awesome was in his office with the door shut, so she did not want to disturb him. Still shaken from last night, she thought about buying a guard dog for protection. *I will pass the idea on to my husband and see what he thinks.*

She went into the kitchen to prepare breakfast and heard Awesome coming. "How was your run?" he asked.

"I feel so much better, but I am still on edge. Maybe we should get a dog to protect the house."

"Sweetie, we are both busy people. Who has time to take care of a dog? You travel a lot. I plan to go back to the shop soon. I thought you wanted an alarm system installed."

"I am so flustered. The thought of someone breaking into our home is frightening. I am at the point where I do not want to be alone in this house any longer."

"Listen to me. There is no need to be petrified. In all probability, kids came into this house. There was no sign of a forced entry. Nothing is missing, and my office was the only place turned inside out. I just received a call from a client who said some kids threw raw eggs at his house because he refused to give them treats."

"But we were not home for anyone to ask us for treats."

"And that is probably why they came into an empty house. Nowadays, these kids are precocious. Why waste eggs or toilet paper when they can just look under the mat, take the key, let themselves in and create mayhem? If you want an alarm system, I will check into it, but maybe you should think long and hard before purchasing a canine."

"Awesome, you are probably right. I am making a mountain out of a molehill. Perhaps, teens did break in. I feel so much better."

"Good, let us eat."

Chapter 53

One week before Thanksgiving, Webster e-mailed Mary Bailey to let her know he would purchase both properties and wanted her agency to manage them.

Mary was elated and needed the following information: a letter of credit from his banks, a financial report from his accountant, his credit score, and two references: one personal and one business. She also wanted to meet with his lawyer.

Webster had everything ready. Boris would represent him, and someone else would be the bogus accountant. Getting two people to submit references would not present any problems. Of course, Webster did not intend to buy those two houses. It was a diversion. He sent the following e-mail to Mary:

My lawyer will be calling you after Christmas. As we agreed earlier, he will handle the wiring of the money into your offshore account.

Mary replied with a follow-up:

I am looking forward to meeting with your lawyer and will provide him with the routing and account number to our offshore bank.

This is all Webster needed: The Baileys' overseas account information. He already knew how to hack into their USA bank accounts.

Meanwhile, Awesome was making plans to sell the shop, which would not be a problem since he was the rightful owner.

Christine was no longer fearful being alone in the house. Awesome had an alarm system put in to placate her. Not that it really mattered, because the system was an imitation.

In three weeks, he would be leaving the country and said, "Christine, on December 21, I will be going out of town on business and will return on January 5." On his last day, he would take her out for brunch to celebrate her birthday, drive her back home, call a cab, and take off for the airport. His flight would leave from LaGuardia Airport at 2 p.m.

On his laptop, Webster had a device that would steal all of the Baileys' money, which would go into a phony bank. After receiving the funds, the money would go to another bank under a different name and account number. Within twenty-four hours, all transactions would evaporate, leaving no paper trail.

Webster would also hack into the title company that registered the Baileys as the titleholders of all their properties; he would have their names removed and replaced with bogus monikers. It would seem as though the Baileys were operating a fraudulent real estate company, selling properties they never bought or owned.

Awesome found a buyer for *Second Hand Treasures* and the building. He wanted three million dollars. The buyer agreed, paid cash and would take over the shop after January 1, 2009.

On the morning of December 21, Christine received a frantic call from a friend who was facing a Catch-22. A new owner purchased the building where her business was located, negated her lease with the prior owner and wanted a one hundred percent rent hike.

The entrepreneur had one week to sign a new lease or the owner would evict her. She wanted Christine to act as a mediator and convince the new proprietor to put together a reasonable lease agreement. The business was in Atlantic City, a two-hour trip by car.

Christine was in a quandary. In several hours, Awesome was leaving for a business trip. She wanted to spend time with him before he left. He was also going to take her out for a bite to eat before heading to the airport. Since time was of the essence, she would have to leave as soon as possible.

She gently woke him. "Awesome, I am sorry to wake you, but I have bad news and will not be able to have brunch or celebrate my birthday with you. A business associate just called; she is about to lose her space due to an increase in rent. I will have to leave for New Jersey."

"How long will you be gone?" he asked.

"I don't know how long it will take to straighten out this mess."

"My little birdie, do not worry. We will have plenty of time to be together. Where will you be staying?"

"I will call an old schoolmate; she and her husband own a bed and breakfast."

"Aren't you afraid she may contact your parents?"

"No, she has never met my parents."

Wow! She has a friend who never met her parents. Who knew?

Christine packed enough items for two days. However, she could not leave without getting some liquid love. Awesome was more than happy to indulge her. They did their fifteen minutes of lovemaking. She then showered and dressed and was ready to leave.

Awesome had a bright idea. "Since we both will be out of town, why don't you stay at the inn until January 5? This way, you will not have to be alone in this house."

"That is a splendid idea. I have not seen my college roommate since graduation. We will have plenty of catching up to do." She kissed and wished him a Merry Christmas, Happy Kwanzaa and a Joyous New Year. She got into her car, and drove off, thinking they would see each other on January 5, 2009.

As he stood at the gate, Awesome waved goodbye to Christine and hurried back into the house. *It was a good ride while it lasted.*

From his disposable cell phone, he moved all of the money from the joint, business, checking and savings accounts from his two banks, while Webster removed all of the money from the Baileys' accounts and into the made-up bank that he had created. The two stole over one billion dollars. Upon arrival to their destination, they would divide the money between them.

Awesome, whose fake passport listed him as Lester Moore, and his pal Webster flew to Zanzibar and would lie low until they were ready to leave for the Caribbean.

Chapter 54

On December 23, a major weekly newspaper received an anonymous letter asking them to investigate the Baileys. The nameless individual enclosed evidence that would assert the couple was operating a shady real estate business and never owned any of the properties they claimed or sold. Instead, they created false titles and deeds and sold those properties to unsuspecting buyers.

The columnist who received the letter was not sure what to make of the volatile story. Going up against the Baileys could destroy the writer's career. She was the one who wrote about their daughter's meltdown at the reception back in May, and the Baileys did not take too kindly to her article.

She would have to tread cautiously before making any final decisions and decided to check with the editor; he examined the letter and the documents and concluded, "Everything looks authentic but get in touch with the Baileys first and get their side of the story."

Getting the couple's side of the allegations was too late. Several online publications broke the story, which spread to major social media and video streaming sites. Many of the printed society and community papers picked up the piece, and it became their front-page news.

Gossip about the Baileys was spreading faster than the common cold. Individuals who purchased their homes from the couple were wondering where they stood when it came to ownership. "Do I really own my home? How could such a seemingly honest couple be so deceitful? Will I lose my house? Will I get my money back?"

The scandal hit business people just as hard. They stood to lose millions of dollars from their dealings with the Baileys. Most were leasing spaces in what they thought were the couple's commercial buildings. These enterprises were now in limbo.

People were beginning to treat the Baileys like pariahs. Those who were once their bosom friends and associates were beginning to distance themselves from the couple.

Members of the church, where the Baileys attended, voted to remove the couple from the board of trustees.

Politicians were no longer interested in working with or seeking the couple's support or funding.

The couple, who was now in a state of confusion, could not believe what people were writing and saying about them.

"These are all lies," James said. "We are upstanding people and would never do something so detrimental that would destroy lives. We uplift folks not bring them down."

"We know who is behind this cock-and-bull story; it is that loathsome Awesome Petté," Mary asserted. "You find him, and the truth will come to light."

If the Baileys thought Awesome Petté was going to be their whipping boy, they would learn that their power, money, and influence would not shield them from what was about to come.

Chapter 55

Two days after Christmas, Christine solved the dilemma facing her client and was able to get the proprietor to put together an equitable ten-year lease.

Thinking about Awesome, she called him on her cell phone but there was no signal. *I will try later. He is probably out of range, or maybe he is in a dead zone.*

She and the owner of the inn caught up on old times. The bed and breakfast was one of the stops made by a sightseeing company and included lunch and a tour of the house, which the proprietor and her husband purchased three years ago.

Christine's conversations with the owners gave her an idea. She would buy the condominium from her parents and turn it into a visitor's stopover; she felt people making New York one of their destinations for business or pleasure would enjoy staying at the unit, which provided privacy, access to the kitchen, cable TV, high-speed internet, parking, gym, spa and other amenities.

In addition, the neighborhood was close to high-end shops, restaurants, sites of interests, buses and subway lines. Brooklyn was becoming the next Manhattan, which Christine would use as a selling point.

Since she was on the outs with her parents, she would let a real estate broker submit an anonymous bid for the condominium. Christine could not wait to share her vision with Awesome.

New Year's Eve was a night to remember. The TV was on, and everyone was waiting for the ball to drop in Times Square. At the stroke of midnight, a festive Christine directed everyone to sing *Auld Lang Syne*.

As happy as she was, an ominous sensation took over her body. Unexpectedly, she could not hear anyone's voice. It was as if she had an outer body experience, which lasted for sixty-seconds. "Are you all right?" one of the guests asked. There was no response.

"Christine, what's wrong?" the owner asked, snapping her fingers.

Ultimately, she came out of her trance. "What happened?" Christine asked.

"It seemed as though you were under some type of spell," the owner's husband said.

"This is a first for me," Christine said. "I saw your mouths moving but could not hear what you were saying. It was as though I was on the outside looking in, but I could not talk or move."

"It must have been all of the excitement," someone said.

"I probably had too much to drink; forgive me for my conduct," a self-conscious Christine said.

"No need to express regret. You are among friends. It could have happened to anyone of us."

"Or maybe it did, and we can't remember," one of the guests said, laughing. Then everyone started to roar with laughter.

It was after 3 a.m. when Christine turned in. She wondered what Awesome was doing and almost made that call but changed her mind. *He is most likely asleep. I will call him later*. Yet, she was starting to question why she had not heard from him on such a celebratory day.

Chapter 56

Complaints against the Baileys were on the rise. The couple decided it was time to stay out of sight until authorities completed their investigation. They could not leave town, talk or answer any questions without their attorney being present.

The couple was desperate. Although Mary fired Danny, she went along with James and decided to rehire him to check out those false allegations made against them.

But Danny Mayo pulled a fast one. He destroyed all information in his computer, cleared out his office and disappeared. He did some underhanded work for the

Baileys, and he was not going to take the fall for any of their crimes.

When Mary discovered Danny was gone, and no one had a clue as to where he was, she suspected he was working with Awesome Petté.

Yet, the biggest shock came when the Baileys tried to withdraw money from all of their USA bank accounts, but the accounts were empty. When that information came out, everyone suspected the couple moved their money into a foreign account. When officials went to check, the overseas account was drained too.

The couple was facing several counts of fraud, larceny, and identity theft. But charging them was not going to be an easy task. No records pertaining to their enterprises in New York State were on file with any of the city, state or federal agencies. It was as though the Baileys and their companies never existed.

It was beginning to look as though Mary and James would never see a courtroom or a prison cell. The DA's office felt some international crime syndicate was out to destroy the couple. After all, they had more enemies than friends.

There were reports that a mysterious organization, operating outside of the USA, had hacked into computers of wealthy citizens, stole important data and sold it to illegitimate groups. They were also responsible for exhausting funds out of corporate bank accounts. Somehow, law enforcement and bank officials were unable to find the villains responsible for these crimes or locate the stolen money.

Not all is lost, James thought. His businesses in Atlanta were unscathed from the allegations. A consortium owned his companies; he and his wife were never listed as owners, and their names never appeared on any corporate documents. Moreover, the couple believed that once Christine found out about their predicament, she would help them by tapping into her trust fund.

Chapter 57

On January 3, Christine still could not reach Awesome. Every time she tried, there was no signal. She was starting to worry. *Something must have happened.* She did not have his itinerary. For all she knew, he was on Mars expanding his business.

She attempted to call the shop but got no answer. It was strange, because Saturday was usually the busiest day.

Maybe the manager closed the shop, she thought.

Many people probably were still celebrating the advent of 2009. The last thing they thought about was buying junk, especially if they were suffering from a hangover.

Since she and Awesome were coming home on the fifth, she would wait then and find out why she had trouble getting in touch with him.

Christine arrived home around ten in the morning but did not know Awesome's incoming flight number or arrival time. If anyone knew, it would be the manager.

She called the shop but heard the following recording: "The number you are trying to reach is no longer in service."

The number is no longer in service. How can that be? She was at a loss and decided to go to *Second Hand Treasures*. When she arrived at the shop, she noticed a signed in the window that read: *The shop is under new management and will reopen on January 19.*

Confused, she stood there and wrote down the telephone number that was on the sign. When she got home, she called that number. A woman answered, "*Antiques Unlimited*, how may I assist you?"

Antiques Unlimited, what in the hell is going on here.

"Hello, this is Christine Petté. I am calling about *Second Hand Treasures*, which my husband owns, but the post in the window says the shop is under new management."

"That is correct," the woman said. "Mr. Petté sold the building along with the business on December 15, 2008. *Second Hand Treasures* is now *Antiques Unlimited*."

Christine was stunned. "How could that be? He never told me he was selling the business. May I have the name of the person who made the purchase?"

"That is something you will have to discuss with Mr. Petté. I am not at liberty to provide any additional information."

As Christine was about to say something, there was a click on the other end. When she called back, there was a busy signal.

When Awesome gets home, he will have a lot of explaining to do.

Christine had fallen asleep on the sofa. It was near two in the morning when she opened her eyes. She heard noises coming from upstairs. "Awesome, is that you?" She ran up the stairs and into the bedroom. It was the trees thumping against the windows.

Again, she tried calling him. Still, there was no signal; her mind started drifting. *Why did I not think of this earlier? Most likely, his schedule is on his calendar or in his computer.* She dashed back downstairs and went into his office. What she was about to discover would leave her questioning her sanity.

Chapter 58

The Baileys would not face any criminal charges. The couple demanded that all publications recant what they had written or face a suit for defamation, but they really had no supporting arguments because the word *allegedly* appeared in every article.

For all purposes, Mary and James were flat broke and busted, but they could not comprehend why their daughter had not contacted them during their time of need.

In times of trouble, we stick together and help each other, Mary thought. *No matter how angry we are, blood is thicker than water*. These were the principles they expected Christine to honor.

Folks who the Baileys once supported financially were avoiding the couple like the plague. People who were once their friends were no longer speaking to them or answering their phone calls for help.

"If their daughter did not come to their aid, why should anyone else reach out to the Baileys," many felt. Of course, there were those who believed karma does not show mercy to anyone who is mean-spirited, deceitful and underhanded.

Mary and James decided to move to Atlanta. His family was able and willing to assist them. There, they would start over. When it came to their daughter, they disowned her. "She made her bed, and she will lie in it with that evil Awesome Petté," her mother said.

Chapter 59

As Christine walked into Awesome's office to check his calendar, she was distracted by a wooden box on his desk. To her, it was magical, with its sparkling stones and attractive designs. She read the card. Beset by past events, she completely forgot about her birthday, the day she and Awesome left on their separate trips.

She searched high and low for a key to open the box. As luck would have it, there was no key. She found a business card with the name *Ray's Locksmith Service* and made that call. "I have a chest, which is missing a key."

"Well, you have called the right place. If it has a keyhole, I can probably open it. Would you like to bring it in? Or I can come to you."

"I will come to you. The box is not heavy."

It was a fifteen-minute ride from her home to the locksmith, which was not too far from Awesome's former shop. As Christine entered the site, a woman approached her. "Good morning, may I help you."

"Yes, thank you. Earlier, I spoke to someone about finding a key to open this chest."

"Oh, you must have spoken to my husband, Ray. He just stepped out. If you like, you can leave the chest along with your name and number, and he will call you if he finds a key."

"How long does it usually take to locate a key?"

"It depends on the make of the box and the type of keyhole. Looking at this box, it could take anywhere from one to three days or maybe longer." The gems mesmerized the woman who was almost lost in thought. "If he does not have a key, he can probably make one for you."

Christine left the box and her contact information.

An hour later, Ray returned to the shop. "A woman came in with this box seeking a key," his wife said. He looked at the box, laughed and jumped for joy. "What are you so happy about?" she asked.

He was tripping over his words. When he looked at the receipt, he could not believe his eyes. "Well, wonders never cease to amaze me."

"What do you mean?"

"Baby doll, this box is going to make us rich. I must leave and will be back in a couple of hours."

With the box, he got into his van and drove to Manhattan to meet with a man who knew how to smuggle precious stones through unlawful channels.

"I have a box that will be of interest to your connections. Look at the stones," Ray said with enthusiasm.

With his magnifying tool, the man examined the gems, but a look of anger overcame him. "Why do you waste my time with such junk? What type of fool do you take me for?"

"What do you mean? I saw this box in a catalog and the stones are worth millions of dollars," Ray said.

"Are you kidding me? You idiot! These are fakes." He threw the box at Ray. "Leave at once before I do something that we will both regret, the man said, seething.

How could this be? He is wrong. Ray decided to go to a certified gemologist.

"These are nothing more than cut glass," the expert said.

Ray left feeling like a complete fool and thought, *Awesome must have substituted the real stones with these phony ones*. Upset, he returned to the shop.

"Well, are we rich yet?" his wife asked in a cynical tone.

"Call Mrs. Petté and tell her there is no key for her chest. I will not be able to make a key for her."

The next day, Christine picked up the box. Even though there was no key, the chest still had an air of the unknown. She would place it on the coffee table. *When Awesome returns home, I will thank him in my own special way.*

Christine had not been out of the house since she went to pick up the box from the locksmith, which was three days ago. She still had not heard from Awesome, did not know any of his friends and had no idea where his parents were.

She decided to go for a walk and ran into a member of the church that she and her parents attended. "Christine, it is so nice to see you. I am so sorry to hear about the legal problems your parents are facing."

"What legal problems?" she asked. "I haven't spoken to them for a while."

"Child, don't you read the newspapers." After the woman explained what had happened, Christine was speechless.

Without saying another word, she left the woman standing on the corner, ran back home and went online. Her parents' troubles were there for the world to see, and they were now financially ruined.

She quickly called them, but the phone was no longer in service. She left the house, got into her car and drove to her parents' home. When she arrived at their house, there was a lock box on the doorknob. The next-door neighbor came out and said, "The Baileys no longer live there. They moved to Atlanta."

Christine went back home. She made a call to Georgia and got her father's sister. "Hi, auntie, this is Christine."

"Where on earth have you been? We have been trying to call you, but your number was not in service," her aunt said in a livid pitch.

"I have been away on business and just found out about my parents' legal and financial troubles."

"What about that husband of yours? He could have called."

"He was also out of town on business."

"Really...! Your parents are staying at a business associate's penthouse. We are very disappointed in you. That performance you did at the reception was a disgrace.

Your mom and dad have done so much for you, and this is how you repay them by being a disrespectful ingrate."

"Now you listen! My parents did not show any respect for my husband; they treated him as if he were a bothersome tick. If they want respect, they must give it." There was a click at the other end of the phone. "Hello, hello."

Christine redialed the number but got the voice mail. Rather than leave a nasty message, she realized she no longer had a family but was thankful that Awesome was in her life.

Feeling awful, she thought long and hard about her parents' situation. She had to do something. Leaving them in an indeterminate state would not be the right thing to do. As her aunt said, "Your mom and dad have done so much for you." They did, sending her to the finest schools, which many parents would have sacrificed their last dollar or would have eaten husks and herring scales to provide such an opportunity for their child.

Christine thought about what her aunt said. Coming to a decision, she would send some money to her parents.

First thing in the morning, she would go to the bank and have a five million dollar cashier's check made out to her parents and send it in the care of her aunt since Christine did not know where her parents were staying.

The money should help get them back on their feet, she thought.

The next morning, Christine went to the bank and asked the clerk to make out a check for five million dollars to Mary and James Bailey. The funds would come from the joint account. The teller looked into the computer and said, "Mrs. Petté, the account is empty."

Christine thought she had misunderstood what the woman said. "Excuse me, over thirty million dollars is on that account. Please, check again."

"Mrs. Petté, the account is empty."

"No! You are mistaken. I had thirty million dollars transferred into this joint account last year. My husband is the other account holder."

"Mrs. Petté, all the money was moved from this account on December 21, 2008."

"That's impossible! I never moved any money from this account."

"Your husband must have moved the money."

Christine started to feel lightheaded. "I want to speak to the manager."

The bank executive came over. "How may I be of assistance to you?"

"I have a joint account with my husband. There should be over thirty million dollars in that account. The teller just told me the account is empty. Can you explain to me how this could have happened?"

The administrator checked the computer and brought up the Pettés' account records. "According to the information on our mainframe, either you or your husband moved the money from all of the accounts, but our records do not show where the money went."

"I never moved any money, and I am sure my husband did not either."

"Did you or your husband give the password to anyone?"

"Of course not," she said in an incensed tone. "We would never give out such personal information to anyone. Just my husband and I have the codes."

"Well, if you did not move the money, then it must have been your husband. Have you checked with him?"

Christine sat there in a stupor. "Perhaps you are right. My husband probably moved the money. He is out of town and is expected back soon."

"Mrs. Petté, if there is nothing else, I must attend to another customer. If you need additional help or have any questions, we are here to help."

"Thank you." She left the bank, returned home, folded herself in a fetal position, and wept until there were no more tears to shed.

Chapter 60

It did not take long for Christine to realize that the most diabolical person she had ever encountered swindled her and most likely her parents out of their wealth. As she was looking back, all the signs were there in plain sight. How she could have missed them was beyond her grasp.

My parents were accurate about Awesome. He was a master charlatan, who captivated my heart and soul like the devil draws in an unsuspecting disciple.

In the same predicament as her parents, she felt trapped in a tangled web. She could not contact them, because they had written her out of their lives and vice versa.

She was too embarrassed to get in touch with her friends or business associates; they would probably turn their backs on her now that she was as penniless as her parents were.

Besides, many of them saw her as unappreciative for not coming to her parents' assistance, not aware that the same person who defrauded her parents also fleeced Christine out of her millions.

She had many obstacles to face. The house was not hers because only Awesome's name was on the deed. What made it even worse, she provided him with the means to take over the house by paying off all of his parents' debts and taxes. Then, she wondered how his parents fitted into this travesty. *They were probably in on the scheme.*

Christine had to make some tough decisions. It was obvious to her that Awesome was gone for good. She would have to consult with a lawyer about ending the marriage and figuring out how to get the house into her name since the property was not part of the marital assets.

The condominium, which she was planning to purchase from her parents, was never going to happen; she was bankrupt and her parents' names did not appear on the deed, which was now in a fuzzy state.

If Christine thought things could not get more muddled, she would discover occurrences that would make her question: *What type of monster did Lupé and Josephina create?*

Christine's divorce lawyer did not foresee any problems getting the marriage dissolved and would file the papers claiming abandonment. Since no one knew where Awesome was, and he could not be located to contest the divorce, the marriage would end immediately.

As far as the house was concerned, problems were beginning to emerge. "Did you know your parents once owned the building that housed the Laundromat that your in-laws owned?" the lawyer asked.

"What? This is news to me." Being away at school most of the time, she may not have known all of the properties her parents actually held. "They must have known who the Pettés were. It is not a name that one would easily forget."

The lawyer stressed, "Many owners do not manage their buildings; they usually hire property managers. Your parents probably never even met your husband's parents, because the building was registered in a foreign country and administered by an overseas conglomerate."

Christine thought that was strange. Her parents were hands-on business people. They would have never allowed anyone to oversee their properties unless they were family.

"There is something else you need to know. My paralegal did a thorough search on Lupé and Josephina Petté. They did not come up in any of the searches. As to whether they were prior owners of the house, nothing showed in any of the title-holding companies. It is as though the couple never existed, and details about the house were expunged from the system."

Christine sat there as though someone had hit her in the head with a wrecking ball. "That is impossible. I saw the deed with his parents' names. They even sent documents signing the house over to their son. In order to get the house into his name, he went to City Hall and filed a quitclaim deed. Wait. A mortgage company sent a letter to Awesome's parents notifying them that they were in arrears. They even owed back taxes on that house."

"Okay, I will need to see all of those documents before I can help you obtain that house. If there is nothing else, I am going to have my paralegal check that quitclaim form your husband completed and filed with the city."

Chills ran up Christine's spine, and the hairs on the back of her neck were rigid. "I can bring those documents to you on Monday. How does nine in the morning sound?"

"That is perfect. I will see you then, Mrs. Petté."

When Christine arrived home, she went through Awesome's office, but deep down in her heart, she knew those papers were gone. To prove her claim, all she had were the letters from the finance company, notices from the tax agencies and copies of the checks she wrote to each entity.

Christine returned to the lawyer's office on Monday.

"Do you have the papers I requested?" the lawyer asked.

"I only have my papers. I could not find my husband's files. He must have taken everything with him, just like his parents did when they left."

"Do you know where his parents are?"

"No. In 2007, I hired a PI to find them, but he had no luck. My husband told me they were born in Guadeloupe, but as it turns out, they were born in Martinique but worked in Guadeloupe before coming to America."

"I will have my assistant check into that. It should not take long to find out where his parents are from or where they are now. Can you tell me when his parents arrived in the USA?"

"It was 1978."

"What year was your husband born?"

"He was born in 1980."

"Do you know which city, state and hospital?"

"He was born in New York, but he never mentioned the hospital."

"I will need his social security number."

Christine sat there with a blank stare. "I do not remember."

"The number would be on your marriage certificate. I assume your husband went to school here. Can you tell me which schools he attended?"

"No."

"How well did you know your husband?" the attorney asked with an intrusive gawk.

"Apparently, I did not know him as well as I thought." She felt like the lawyer was interrogating her in a courtroom and chastising her for not taking the time to do a thorough background check on Awesome Petté.

If being dumb was a crime, I would be serving a life sentence, Christine thought.

"I will go over the papers you submitted and get back to you in a couple of days. In the meantime, if you can think of anything that can help me get that house in your name, call me."

"Thank you, I will."

Christine was now in a state of turmoil. She was living in a mansion that did not belong to her. The business she financed, as a silent partner, was under new ownership. She had to find a way to pay off all the invoices that Awesome racked up while running the shop.

Seen as an astute businessperson, she could not fathom how a seemingly charming man was capable of manipulating her and committing such shocking offenses.

It is understandable why my parents disowned me. I brought such shame to the Bailey name. People will never see me or my family in the same light.

Christine was never one to seek revenge against anyone who wronged her or her parents. Her mom and dad, especially her mom, were masters when it came to settling scores, rightfully or not. Yet, she could not call on them for help. She was alone and would have to seek reprisal on her own. What she did not realize then was that her dire situation was about to take an out of the blue turn.

Chapter 61

The lawyer called Christine with good news and bad news. "The good news is your husband's parents did own the house. They obtained a loan from *Home Financial Services*, which submitted the certificate to a title-holding company, but the title company maintained they never received the document."

"And what is the bad news?" Christine asked, crossing her fingers.

"Awesome does not own the house. Even though he filed a quitclaim document, which the clerk could not find, it is invalid since we have no proof that his parents actually signed over the house to him."

"What do we do now?" an anxious Christine asked.

"Can you come to my office tomorrow at noon? We will discuss your options."

"Yes, I will see you then."

When Christine woke up the next day, it was six in the morning. Noon could not have come fast enough for her. She was too nervous to eat breakfast and decided to sit in the garden and go online.

While surfing the Internet, she thought about Awesome. Unknowingly, she contributed to his deception by ignoring the warning signs. On top of that, she paid off his debts, poured money into his business, but she ended up being a liability.

It was near eleven when Christine ended her one-woman pity party. She showered and dressed, got into her car and drove to the lawyer's office.

"Good afternoon, Mrs. Petté. It is nice to see you."

"It is nice to see you too."

"I would like to discuss what we can do regarding the house. Because we cannot find the Pettés, I can file a document claiming the owners have abandoned the property. You paid the arrears and back taxes, so that works in your favor. There is only one problem: If the Pettés resurface, they can evict you or put the house up for sale."

"If they never come back, will I still be able to stay in the house?" Christine asked, hoping the answer would be yes.

"Yes, but you will not be the owner until you receive the deed to the house. It will take up to ninety days to file and process the papers."

Taking a gulp of fresh air, Christine would have to make a decision. "Does this mean that once I get the deed, the house is mine, and the Pettés, if they decide to come back, cannot make a claim to the property?"

"That is correct. They may choose to go to court, but they will not have a leg to stand on."

"Go ahead and file the papers."

Three months later, Christine received her divorce papers and the deed to the house. She was now the official owner and could sell or lease the estate. The house was appraised at 2.5 million dollars.

After careful deliberation, she decided to sell the manor. As much as she loved the place, living there was no longer practical. The cost to maintain that house was costly, and the painful memories of Awesome's betrayal were too much for her to bear.

Christine did find a buyer. Her asking price was three million dollars, which included all the furnishings and Awesome's two vehicles and other add-ons.

One month later, she purchased a one-bedroom condominium in Park Slope. The unit came with two attic spaces and a two hundred square feet terrace. The price tag was eight hundred-fifty thousand dollars.

By the end of 2009, things were beginning to look up for Christine. She went back to using her maiden name. Old clients were starting to come back. Because of the downturn, more people were seeking her advice on starting their own business or trying to stay afloat with the business they owned.

She had not spoken to her parents. There were rumors that they were filing for divorce. That did not surprise Christine. She always wondered what they actually saw in each other. It was obvious to her, that behind locked doors, there was never any genuine love or passion in that marriage.

What really piqued her interest was the identity of her real father. She would hear murmurs among strangers, friends, and relatives that James was not her biological father, but Reverend Christopher Dune was.

How people came to that conclusion always amused her. She knew Pastor Dune was not her father because his wife insisted he take a DNA test to squash those tales. After graduating from college, Christine and the Pastor went to a diagnostic clinic for testing. The results were conclusive. He was not her biological father.

She never let on to her parents about taking the test. Pretending that James Bailey was her father was supposed to be acceptable. As to whether James was her true father, did not matter to Christine now. The fact that he denounced her said it all.

Chapter 62

Awesome and Webster left Zanzibar and flew to the Cayman Islands, which would be their permanent place of residence. They each opened an account at different banks and deposited a little over five hundred-fifty million dollars. Awesome purchased a two-bedroom house overlooking the ocean. Webster went for a one-bedroom villa in the bustling city.

To celebrate their windfall, the two decided to meet and go to a bar, where the locals and tourists gathered. On this particular evening, the place was half-full.

"We finally hit it big," Awesome said.

"Yes, and without much effort," Webster said. "And to think we owe it all to your clueless wife and her muckety-muck parents. We have enough money to last several lifetimes."

"That is wonderful music to my ears, Mr. Manny Smith."

"For now, I think I will stick with Webster Jones."

"Do you think I should continue to go by the name Lester Moore?"

"You know the answer to that question? The name Awesome Petté would stick out like a woman's hair on fire. You never know who is still searching for you. No one is going to be looking for a Lester Moore."

"Yeah, you are probably right."

The two were chatting and enjoying their drinks. Suddenly, a woman, wearing a red see-through dress, came sashaying into the tavern, sat down at a corner table and ordered a cocktail. The dimmed lights concealed her face.

She sat there for fifteen minutes, gawking at Awesome and Webster. After finishing her drink, she got up, walked past their table and said, "Enjoy your evening, gentlemen."

Surprised, both men looked up. They never really noticed the woman when she came into the bar. "Who in the devil was that?" Awesome asked.

"Hell, if I know," Webster replied. "I never saw her come in."

"I did not see her either," Awesome said. "We must be losing our footing to have missed her."

But, something about that woman did not sit well with them. A bizarre feeling began to overtake their bodies.

"That was weird," Webster said.

"It sure was. It was as though a whiff of wickedness swept past us," Awesome said. They looked at each other, laughed and contributed their emotions to the woman's remark and her imposing red dress.

"Let's follow her and see where she goes," Webster suggested.

"That's a good idea." When they got outside, the woman was nowhere to be found. "I guess it is safe to say that neither one of us is going to get lucky tonight," Awesome said, laughing. They went back in and ordered more drinks.

Awesome and Webster decided to go to another bar, which had more customers and plenty of hotties. They met some women, chatted with them but decided leaving them there was better than bringing them home. Not really acclimated to their new environment, they did not want to draw too much attention.

With all of their money, they still had to be extra careful when it came to letting strangers into their lives. They cut off all contacts with their associates back in the USA. No one knew where Awesome and Webster were, and they wanted to keep it that way.

It was around 3 a.m. when the two left the tavern. Since Webster lived nearby, he walked home. Awesome called for a cab and was home in fifteen minutes.

The banging on the door had awakened Awesome at eleven in the morning. It was Webster, yelling and crying, "It's gone; all my money is gone."

"What are you talking about? What money is gone?"

"The money we stole from your wife and her parents."

At first, Awesome thought Webster was suffering from a hangover from all of the drinking last night. "Come in and sit down, and tell me what's going on with you."

"I am trying to tell you! When I went to the bank to withdraw some money, the clerk said, 'You closed your account three days ago.'"

"What did you say!?" Awesome asked in shock. "How on earth did that happen? You would never give your username or password to anyone. Or did you?"

"You know I would never do such a thing. I would not even give that information to my wife if I had one."

"Something is not right," Awesome said, grabbing his laptop. "Maybe I should check my account." He went online, typed in his username and password, but got the following message: *You have entered the incorrect password.* "No….! I have not entered the wrong password." He tried again, but the same message reappeared.

"Awesome, what is it?"

"Webster, I must leave and go to the bank, which is saying I have entered the wrong password. Wait here until I get back. There must be some explanation. Maybe there was a glitch in the system."

He dashed to the bank, which was five blocks from his home. Out of breath, he went to the manager to inquire about his account. When the overseer checked the information provided by Awesome, she said, "Our records do not show you ever having an account at this bank."

Stunned, he shouted, "That is a lie! There is over five hundred million dollars on that account."

"You may have that amount of money in another depository but not here."

"I want to speak to your boss."

"You are speaking to her."

"I am not leaving until that money is on my account," Awesome said, pounding on the desk.

"Sir, you can leave now, or I will have security escort you out of this bank; if you refuse to leave, I will call the police."

The word police calmed Awesome. The last thing he needed was a confrontation with the law. He left the bank and walked back home.

"How did things go at the bank?" Webster asked with a worried look.

"According to the manager, I never had an account at that bank."

"What is going on here? How could both of us lose our money at different banks?"

"That is a good question, Webster. Money does not disappear like that. Maybe you stole my money. To try and throw me off the track, you come up with this trumped-up story making like someone hacked into your account."

"How could you think that? We have been friends forever, always stood by and covered each other's back. Now you are accusing me of betraying you in such a contemptible manner."

"Yes, I am. Who else had the capability of getting into people's accounts and pilfering their money? If you could do that to Christine and her parents, then maybe you did it to me."

"If you really feel that way, we are no longer friends. I am in the same boat as you, destitute." Webster left. To clear his head, he walked home.

Several days later, Awesome thought about what he said to his best and only friend. *How could I have accused him of doing such a horrific act?* He decided to drive to Webster's place and apologize to him.

While driving on an isolated road, his mind went back to the good times he and Webster shared. Without warning, someone dashed in front of his car. He recognized the person and screamed, "Oh my God, it can't be you." In shock, he lost control of the steering wheel. In a matter of seconds, his car swerved off the road and plummeted into a ravine.

Five minutes away from his villa, Webster started to cross the street, but the bright sun blocked his vision. He never saw the oncoming car.

The impact of the motor vehicle sent Webster eight feet into the air. When he landed on the pavement, he was semi-conscious. A few good Samaritans came to his aid. When he looked up, he recognized the individual who was looking down at him. As he was about to say something, Webster slipped into unconsciousness; the ambulance came on the scene and rushed him to the hospital.

Chapter 63

Three days later, some vacationers discovered Awesome's car and called the ambulance. He was still alive; rescuers got to him and rushed him to the medical center. Webster was also a patient there. The medical staff was not aware that the two men knew each other.

Awesome was delirious and could not remember who or where he was. The chart had him listed as Lester Moore. "Mr. Moore, can you hear me? You are in the hospital. You were in a car accident. Some tourists found you in a canyon."

Looking at the doctor, Awesome asked, "Where am I? Where is that person who darted in front of my car?"

"Mr. Moore, what person?" the doctor asked. It was unproductive. Awesome was still rambling about how he swerved his car to avoid hitting a pedestrian.

"It will probably take a day or two before Mr. Moore regains all of his faculties," the head physician said to the medical team.

Because Awesome was wearing his seatbelt, he did not have any internal injuries. He was suffering from dehydration, and his electrolytes were dangerously low. A CAT scan did not indicate any trauma to the head.

On the other hand, Webster suffered broken ribs, legs and arms, and massive spinal and head injuries. Physicians were not sure if he would ever walk again. Since he needed long-term care, he became a resident at a convalescent home.

While Awesome was recuperating, a stranger came into his room. "Last night, a fire destroyed your five million dollar home; fire officials cannot determine if it was arson or defective wiring that caused the blaze."

He recognized the visitor, the one who dashed in front of his car. "How did you find me?" Awesome asked. The individual never answered him, left the room and disappeared.

Awesome quickly got out of his bed, was about to run after the person but an orderly stopped him. "Mr. Moore, where are you going?"

"I am trying to follow that person who was just in my room."

"Mr. Moore, no one came into your room. Visiting hours are over."

"There was someone in here." Suddenly, he jumped the orderly and threw him to the floor. Awesome ran out of the room and into the street, searching for that person.

The orderly notified the staff that Mr. Moore attacked him; two other orderlies joined him to search for the patient. They found him on the beach, where his house once stood.

"I know who set fire to my house. It was..." Before he could give them a name, one of the orderlies injected him with a mild sedative; the other two men placed him into a straight jacket and took him to a psychiatric facility. It was anyone's guess as to how long Awesome would remain there.

Chapter 64

Back in Brooklyn, spring was in full bloom. It was now 2010. Christine's business made close to five hundred thousand dollars in sales. She was now dating, but marriage was something she would never do again.

Her parents did divorce. The last she heard, her mother was living in Sag Harbor. She received a nice divorce settlement, which provided her with the luxury of purchasing a nice townhouse in a gated community, where she enjoyed hobnobbing with the rich, the famous and the infamous.

James bought a home in the Bahamas. He did not intend to return to the United States. The buzz was that he married his mistress whom he met after he married Christine's mother, but no one back home knew the identity of this woman.

Taking the news in stride, Christine was happy for her parents and hoped they would live their lives to the fullest. As she was getting ready to make lunch, the doorman called to inform her that the mail carrier was on his way to her unit to deliver a letter, which came from the Cayman Islands.

Christine did not know anyone on that island. There was no returned name or address. *This is strange*. When she opened the letter, there was a cashier's check for one billion dollars and the following message:

Dear Mrs. Petté:

We have never met, but I had the misfortunate to have met Awesome Petté and his conniving friend, Webster Jones. Just like you, I fell for their charismatic charm and went out of my way to help them achieve their goals. But I was also fooled by them.

Well, I vowed that I would make them pay for the way they treated me and have been watching and studying their every mood. Of course, they had no idea what I was up to, but I knew what they were planning for you.

I tried to warn you about Awesome Petté. I was even at the reception that your parents threw for you and that scoundrel. I even called you several times to caution you.

Awesome's only objective was to get your money. I got back the money that he and his pal stole from you and your parents. How I was able to retrieve the money does not matter.

Hoping this check will help you get back on your feet. When it comes to business, I can see you are a fair and smart woman. Moreover, I am not seeking any rewards. My greatest compensation is that those two rogues will never get the opportunity to hurt another human being.

To say Christine was blown away was accurate. *Who wrote this letter and sent this check? And who is Webster Jones?* She never heard Awesome talk about anyone from his past.

She immediately called the bank where the check was drawn. As to who wrote the check, the bank would not provide that information. All that mattered was that the instrument was authentic.

Christine only kept the money that Awesome stole from her. She would establish a trust fund for each of her parents, divide the remaining money and place half into each of their accounts.

Since she could not explain where the money came from or how it landed at her doorstep, she would let her lawyer get in touch with her parents and give as much details that would satisfy them.

If anyone wanted the answers, they would have to know who wrote that letter and sent that check, and Beatrice Moon, the avenging angel, was never going to reveal herself, because as long as people like Awesome and Webster are out there duping vulnerable women out of their money, she will be there to put forth her style of retribution.

Chapter 65

In 2012, the mansion, which Christine once shared with Awesome, became the subject of an investigation. The owner started to revamp the basement into a two-bedroom apartment.

Behind a partition, the workforce discovered a locked door, broke the latch and entered the room. What they discovered had them shaking in their boots. Two skeletons were huddled in a corner next to a locked safe. The workers notified the owner who called the police.

It did not take long for reporters and TV stations to park in front of that house; they were like turkey buzzards searching for carcasses.

Everyone wanted to know, "Who were those people? Did someone murder them? How long have they been there?" It would take several months before the community got its answers.

The pathologist noted that the pair was a man and a woman. As far as she could tell, they were anywhere from 50 to 60 years of age.

The man died instantly from a massive heart attack. Because the bolt on the door malfunctioned, the woman could not get out of the room to get help. She died from dehydration and starvation. The well-insulated door and walls would have prevented anyone living in that house from hearing her calls for help.

New arrivals in the neighborhood had no idea who the two people were. Older residents guessed that the couple was Lupé Petté and his wife, Josephina.

To make that determination, forensic would have to get DNA from family members. This would be impossible because Awesome disappeared, and Christine never met any of his relatives or knew where they were.

Authorities got into the safe, which contained two passports, a marriage license, birth certificates, school records, a deed to the house and other miscellaneous papers.

According to the Pettés' passports, the couple was from Cayenne, the capital of French Guiana, an overseas department of France, situated on the northeastern coast of South America. But it was later discovered that all the documents were fakes.

Officials from various agencies did a search, but they could not find any verification as to whether the couple was born in Guiana or ever lived there. It was never quite clear how the duo entered the USA, where they really came from, or how they were able to enter the United States, purchase a house and a business with phony credentials.

Currently, several federal agencies are examining all of the contents found in the safe. It is anyone's guess if the truth about the Pettés will ever be revealed.

Yet, neighbors and everyone else still wanted to know, "Where is Awesome Petté?" Forensic would need to find him to compare his genetic material with the couple's DNA.

When Christine got whiff of the news and was questioned by authorities, she was as oblivious as everyone else was about Awesome Petté, and the couple found in the basement. Her mind started racing with questions: *Who was that couple pretending to be the Pettés? Did the bolt on that door really fail or was there some other sinister act at work?*

Since the walls in that house could not talk, Christine came up with her own ending: *The remains were the Pettés, and Awesome locked his parents into that room in order to get his hands on the estate. He then destroyed all documents that would have given authorities clues as to his whereabouts. Awesome, wherever you are, you will suffer the consequences for your vile actions.*

About the Author

Born in 1946, Vivienne Diane Neal is a writer, blogger, and an author. She is a storyteller with a wicked sense of humor, has been writing articles for over thirty years and started penning fictional short stories in 2007. Vivienne gets her story ideas from observing people, places, and things and watching true TV court cases and talk shows.

Her book, **Retribution Unleashed**, ranked No. 66 on UBAWA's (Urban Books, Authors, and Writers of America) top 100 Books of 2013.

Now, semi-retired, she continues to write articles on love, romance, relationships, and other topics of interest on her blog at https://www.oneworldsinglesblog.net.

Comments, feedback, and questions may be sent to info@oneworldsinglesblog.net